Prologue
Grace

According to statistics, 88 percent of people snoop on their ex's at least once following the demise of their relationship. Curiosity is harmless, right? Wrong. Snooping is bad, very, very bad. But do you know what's worse? Breaking the cardinal rule of stalking: don't get caught.

The crime I committed? Social media suicide: accidentally liking my ex's engagement post. Cue sinking so much vodka last night, that I'd be speaking Russian if my tongue wasn't stuck to the roof of my mouth.

Must. Find. Life. Sustaining. Water.

Correction: Must. Pee. Then. Find. Life. Sustaining. Water.

I allow the events of the previous 24 hours to envelope me. Shame? Check. Humiliation? Check. Getting drunk and hooking up with the most comely and handsome guy I ever saw? Oh yes, come to momma, check, check, check. Now, in the grand scheme of things, liking my ex's post doesn't seem like the end of the world. In fact, it turned out therapeutic. If coming explosively three times is therapy, book me in because I require extensive, regular treatment.

So, here I am, enjoying post-orgasmic bliss, wrapped up in a very hot, very naked man. Beside me, on the super king ornate oak bed, lies my hook-up from my Russian vodka - induced evening. Sebastian. Even though my brain is foggy and a thousand drums are beating a symphony of torture inside my head, he's someone I won't be forgetting. He oozes pure, unadulterated, rugged sex appeal. Hard muscles, smooth tan skin, with a bulge beneath the sheets that makes my eyes and mouth water. He is hotter than Jamaica in July, and he is snuffling lightly as he sleeps beside me.

I fleetingly wonder if he was as drunk as I was last night. He didn't seem as drunk, but then I'm probably not the best judge of his drunkenness, considering I thought I was totally sober, as I danced on the bar, taking off my cardigan and flinging it at the dark haired, hot piece of ass that bought me a drink. Not exactly subtle or sophisticated, and definitely not usual Grace-like behaviour, but it helped land me my first ever hook-up. And boy, what a hook-up!

Sebastian's place is fancy. Last night I was too busy performing a very drunken striptease to take in the finer details of his home. His huge bedroom looks like a fifteenth century king lives here. The furniture is all glossy carved oak. We were too frenzied with lust to consider shutting the floor-to-ceiling flock curtains last night, and now the room glows with sunlight so bright that I should probably apply lotion. Strewn from his bedside lamp is my bra, and my skirt hangs from the bedpost. On the floor are Sebastian's jeans and shirt, forming an outline like police tape at a crime scene.

Sebastian's mouth makes a smacking sound, as though he too is thirsty. His dark hair, silkier than the finest satin, is just long enough for my fingers to latch into it and direct his

Operation My Fake Girlfriend

Emily James

Copyright © 2020 Emily James

All rights reserved.

ISBN:9798642520888

Contents

Prologue	1
Chapter 1	6
Chapter 2	16
Chapter 3	27
Chapter 4	41
Chapter 5	53
Chapter 6	68
Chapter 7	78
Chapter 8	84
Chapter 9	90
Chapter 10	100
Chapter 11	108
Chapter 12	113
Chapter 13	121
Chapter 14	129
Chapter 15	134
Chapter 16	138
Chapter 17	146
Chapter 18	150
Chapter 19	159
Chapter 20	163
Epilogue	172
Acknowledgements	178
About the Author	179

Operation: My Fake Girlfriend

mouth exactly where I need it. I flush at the memory. I've never been so vocal before, but my god he was good, and since I told myself this was a one-off, a shag-a-thon to end my long sex sabbatical, I busted out all my best moves and made the most of our encounter. Now, I'm deliciously sore and eager for a repeat performance.

Does a morning-after bang go against hook-up protocol? I'm tempted to text my sister and ask—she's better schooled in subjects such as these—but my phone is in my clutch, which hangs from the corner of Sebastian's wall-size television.

Of course, that's assuming that Sebastian wants a rematch. I have no frame of reference for hook-up etiquette. Should I have left already? Hangover anxiety is creeping in and crushing my buzz. What if he can't remember my name or he asks me what I'm still doing here? More importantly, what if he craves a repeat performance?

With my bladder fit to burst and the fear of morning breath hanging over me, I push his lean forearm—ripped with sinewy muscle—off my stomach and slide across the bed until my toes splay in the plush carpet.

The en suite door creaks as I open it to go deal with my morning breath and haystack hair. The bathroom is opulent, with a floor to ceiling window next to the tub. Outside the sun is shining, and I can see several gardeners tending the sprawling manicured grounds.

Fuck.

Sebastian is rich. Not just rich, loaded.

Last night we steamed up the windows of the taxi—not that I was paying attention to our surroundings. When the cab stopped, Sebastian carried me up the steps to the door and once inside, my sole concern was getting a look at his body, not his house. I had an inkling from his fancy bedroom he had a nice place, but from the view outside the room it's clear I'm in a mansion with sprawling acres of manicured lawns, a winding driveway with a huge, ornate water feature in its middle. Intimidation prickles beneath my skin as I finger brush my teeth and wash away the black half-moons beneath my eyes where my bargain basement "stay-put" mascara bled down my face.

Back in the bedroom, my eyes lock on the perfect muscular curve of Sebastian's ass. His tan is seamless, only marred slightly by the crescent-shaped abrasions from my fingernails as they dug into his flesh.

Sebastian's steady breathing is the only sound until my phone pings from inside my clutch—probably my friend Willow checking what I got up to last night after she went home to relieve her babysitter. I tiptoe across the room to retrieve my bag, admiring the myriad of photos clustered on either side of the television.

Then my breathing stops altogether, and my heart drops into my stomach.

Sebastian in a suit—looking sexier than Channing Tatum naked—is photographed standing in front of Stone Enterprises' head office, aka my new place of work as of two weeks ago.

Besides that is a framed certificate commending Sebastian *Stone* for a charitable donation to Hope for the Homeless. And beneath that is a picture of Arthur Stone, the founder of Stones Enterprises with his arm around Sebastian Stone, his grandson.

Shit!

Sebastian Stone.

Grandson of Arthur Stone.

I one-nighted my boss's, boss's, boss.

It didn't even occur to me to ask him his surname. Although now I wish I asked for his business card, driver's licence, and a semen sample. Scratch that, I got the semen sample, now I just need to figure out how to get out of here before he commits my face to sober memory and recognises me at work.

As if he can hear the fire alarm of panic going off in my head, Sebastian stirs and his hand sweeps across the luxurious ten-thousand-thread-count cotton as though reaching for me. My lady parts zing with desire. I want more. A second helping of the man sweeter than the dirtiest of desserts. I stand naked and torn. Stone Enterprise's has a very strict non-fraternisation policy. And my ex started out as my boss at my last job, and that didn't end well for me. In fact, it ended very badly. I can't go through that again. My eyes flick from Sebastian to the imaginary writing on the wall until defeat washes over me. I just took on a massive mortgage and I can't afford to lose my job again. I have to get out of here. If I fuck and run, maybe Sebastian won't remember my face. Then, when I bump into him at work, which could happen, he'll assume déjà vu and I won't get fired by HR again.

I hunt for my clothes, hastily fastening my bra, unhooking my shirt from beneath the bed, and slipping on my skirt. I scan the room for my knickers. They're not on the floor or the furniture. My heart quickens its pace, and I rub my eyes and complete another scan of the room. For a second I wonder if I left the house yesterday without them, but then I spy them hanging from the chandelier above his bed, precocious like their owner.

Fuck!

Sebastian lets out a light moan and his hand reaches up to rub the tip of his perfectly straight nose. There's no time. Retrieving my knickers without standing on his bed and waking him is impossible. I snatch my peep-toe shoe from beneath the dresser, and the other from on top, sling my clutch beneath my arm, and prepare to do the walk of shame knickerless, panicked about pending unemployment, and mourning my missing morning-after orgasm.

Still, with any luck, I'll get out of here without being seen and I won't run into that sexy bastard ever again.

Chapter 1
Sebastian

Four weeks later

I rarely venture home to Heaven, East Angleford, but with our head of operations at the Heaven branch quitting, I'm based here for the foreseeable future. As the oldest Stone brother and heir to Stone Enterprises, I prefer to work from the office in the city. It's less political than home turf. Yet, I find myself back at Grandpa's sprawling estate at least once a month.

"Didn't think you'd show," my brother Luke says, passing me two-fingers of bourbon.

"Wouldn't miss a summons from Grandpa," I reply giving him a jovial wink. Luke and I complain about the old man and his old-fashioned ways, but it's done with a certain amount of acceptance. He's raised us since our parents died when we were only little kids, and we both respect and admire him. I shoulder nudge Luke and slurp the warm liquid, letting out a sigh as the liquor hits the spot. "Thank you, it's been a bourbon kind of day."

"That bad, huh?" Luke smiles knowingly.

My eyes narrow. "What's the old man told you?"

Luke shrugs, and a look of pure mischief coats his

features.

"You know he's following me on Instagram now, and he doesn't approve of what he sees. My Insta account is not a reflection of the way I conduct business." Grandpa might be looking eighty square in the face but nothing, and I mean nothing, escapes him.

"He's got old-fashioned values, and he has every right to check up on you."

"I'm thirty years-old, Luke. I don't need checking up on and besides, he doesn't check up on you. In fact, you live in the same small town and speak to him less than I do. Seven emails I received from him yesterday. Seven. It's like he doesn't trust me."

"Seb, you know he trusts you or he wouldn't have made you an executive. He doesn't check on me because I chose not to join the family business. Being an ultra-smooth cop is much more my style. But you, you brought this all on yourself, following in his footsteps, and offering yourself up as a young protégé since you were old enough to piss standing up. He's handing you his empire; he'd be mad not to check up on you."

I down the last of my bourbon. He's right, and it sucks.

"Please join us in the dining hall," Betty, my grandpa's maid says, putting on her most proper accent, which is odd to hear, since this is the same woman who sang us lullabies and called us dirty rotten scallywags when we stole her baked cakes right out the oven.

I take a seat at the huge, oval mahogany dining table, opposite Grandpa. Luke flanks me to one side, and it's like I'm four years old all over again and Gramps caught me doodling on the wallpaper.

"Sebastian, you came." My grandpa nods, like he thinks I wouldn't show up today despite never missing family dinner on the last Sunday of every month. Even when I was in college, he'd send the helicopter first thing Sunday morning, no matter how hung over to shit I was, and have me here in time for dinner. "And my dear Luke, I trust you had no difficulty swapping your shift to attend family Sunday? Is it easier now you're a detective on the force?"

"Sure is, Gramps. Got my team now, and I write my own hours," Luke responds energetically, like all his Christmases came around at once.

"And I bet all the women in town are going bonkers over the new detective." I wink at Luke and he gives me a subtle smirk and nods his head from behind his wine glass.

"Always thinking with your privates, Sebastian." My grandfather shakes his head and pulls his napkin onto his lap.

"And what exactly is the problem with a grown man enjoying healthy, consensual sex?"

"There is nothing wrong with the union between a couple in love. Nothing at all. But you're infatuated with your penis, always have been, ever since you learned to use your hands. In fact, I seem to remember a young Sebastian using his best efforts as a toddler to stretch it right into his mouth. It worried your poor mother you'd end up with a neck injury. I'm sure there's even a photograph in an album somewhere. But alas, I digress. Don't you think it's time you grew up?" Gramps looks smug at the mention of the childhood tale that never fails to embarrass me. I shake off his needling. I'm about to argue that I am grown up, he just hasn't noticed, but Gramps doesn't give me a chance. "Now, now, that's quite enough of the trailer park talk. Tell me about Milan."

It's the question I've been dreading, and so I'm pleased when Betty rushes through the swing door to the dining hall, pushing her trolley full of homemade goodness. I'm overwhelmed with scents of beef and spices, probably a half a dozen different side courses, and the best gravy either side of the equator. I pull a sip of the pre-poured red wine in front of me and savour the taste as Betty loads the table. I'm glad of the distraction, though it's too much to hope that Betty's presence will change Grandpa's course of questioning.

When I look up, Grandpa is viewing me curiously. It's hard to tell if the lines around his face are from age or laughter, but beneath his soft, warm exterior is a hardened businessman who knows how to achieve his goals.

Betty loads my plate and gives me a warm smile. "Have you been eating enough? Have some extra potatoes, we need to fatten you up." She loads my plate higher until I hold out a hand to stop her.

"They frown on carbs in L.A." I wink and grin at Betty and she shakes her head, moving to load Luke's plate.

"I trust carbs are permissible in Milan, though, Sebastian? The home of Italian cuisine, fashion, and beautiful, brown-eyed Mediterranean women?" Grandpa's brows raise as if accusatory.

Luke tucks into his meal. He knows he is not the intended recipient of our grandfather's provocative remarks.

"They eat carbs just fine in Milan. Except for the runway models; I believe they prefer tomato salad, with good olive oil, of course." I give Grandpa a courteous grin. If he wants an argument, I won't rise to it.

"And yachts. Million-dollar yachts with playboy heirs running around them like they don't have a care in the world? I believe they're quite partial to those, if the press reports and Instagram are correct," he counters without allowing his tone to reflect the acidity of his comments—for that would not be acceptable dinner party conduct.

I sigh and pinch the bridge of my nose.

"You know I broke the Gino deal while I was there? Fifteen million worldwide followers, all desperate for Gina Gino's designer couture, and I signed her to work exclusively for Stone Enterprises. Or did that go unnoticed?" I fork more food in my mouth, almost expecting it to taste as sour as the conversation. "Thank you, Betty. This is delicious, as always," I add, trying in vain to change the subject. Betty sits farther down the table, as she has always done. At sixty years old, she looks smaller than I remember, less imposing, but still no doubt a force to be reckoned with. Much like my grandpa, Arthur Stone, billionaire entrepreneur of everything textiles. Yet somehow—unlike fashions and trends—the man doesn't age. Okay, so his hair is white, and his face weathered with age. Still, he looks closer to sixty than approaching eighty.

"Sebastian, you were all over the media. Drinking champagne and partying like some kind of college frat boy. Do you understand how damaging that is to the family brand? The brand I built from scratch. It's a mockery, that's what it is." Okay, so Grandpa looks pissed now, as evidenced by him putting down his cutlery and the stern look he's throwing me from his grey, almost opaque eyes.

Luke sighs from the corner of his mouth and turns the conversation to Betty. "Is the beef from the Davenport farm?" he asks. "I've sure missed your cooking."

While I appreciate my brother's attempt to deflect the tension, my gramps lack of trust raises my hackles and I wonder, since he still works a sixty-hour week, if he has any intention of handing over the company he's been promising me since I was fifteen. His eightieth birthday is in just over a month, and I hope that is when he will hand over the reins but he hasn't even mentioned it.

Before Betty has a chance to answer, my silver cutlery slam on the mahogany. "The problem with you, old man, is that you don't understand how things work these days. I have to schmooze with the clients. Offer them advantages they don't get with other suppliers and investors. If Stone Enterprises is to move with the times, we have to have interests in other avenues. Like my idea for the hospitality industry—"

Air whooshes against my skin as my grandfather slams his fist on the table. "That idea was cheapening to the brand!"

Luke's hand goes to massage his temple in a movement that is pure WTF. At me? At Gramps? Who knows, but he won't be happy our family meal has turned into a tit-for-tat.

"It was a conglomerate of hotel chains with sales worth three-point-four-million," I seethe through gritted teeth.

My grandpa lifts his cutlery, as though mentally shrugging off my efforts. "It was a two-bit chain offering happy hour for truckers and not something I want Stone Enterprises associated with. The long-term damage would have been catastrophic," he says dismissively—like he's telling his seven-year-old grandson, not the thirty-year-old man in front of him. It stings. It stings like every single other thing he told me I knew was right. I've been trying so hard to get his approval and failing that I don't know which way is up anymore. "You've done well in certain aspects. The Milan deal was a good one," he says as though patting me on the head. "But I know you can do better. The next arm of the company rests on your shoulders."

Grandpa's been saying this since I was fifteen and showed an interest in the family business. It was easy for Luke, he always wanted to be a cop. I fell into the business, yet it feels like it's getting farther and farther away from me.

"You need to shift focus and clean up your act. I've seen you on Insta. All the parties and half-naked models. What do you think that says about the future of Stone Enterprises, huh?" He doesn't wait for my answer as he judiciously slides his cutlery in the centre of his plate. "Where there's no family, there's no future," he says firmly.

"I didn't sleep with any of those models. And they offered it up, a lot! You don't have the slightest idea of Insta and social media, and what's current. Without the parties, models and followers, we are just another stale brand that will lose its edge on the market!" I try to tell him, but he shakes his head as though I'm trying to persuade him to have a side of magic mushrooms. If he only knew how bored I have become with the parties and the lifestyle. These days it feels like the same shit, just a different day.

"You do not need to tell me about social media. I snappy chat, tweet, and text. That model from last week had a six-in-a-bed scandal! I ask myself: How do six people even manage it?"

"You probably don't want to know, Gramps," Luke chimes in. "But if ever you're curious, you want to check out www—"

"For fucks sake, Luke, don't start giving him porn sites to cruise." I drop my cutlery on my plate and my hand flies to my face, because if there's anything that'll put you off prime sirloin beef, it's the image of your grandfather cruising the internet for porn.

Gramps sighs. "Do you want the business, Sebastian?"

I nod. I've spent the past fifteen years working towards this goal. I've networked my way into every top fashion house and brought the Stone name into the twenty-first century, not that my grandfather appreciates that.

"Well, I want family morals. Show me you care about someone more than you do the business. Show me you have more invested in this company than a pay check. A legacy, that's what I want to see from you boys."

Luke's head raises up like a meerkat. His hand goes to his chest and his innocent, younger brother eyes pop out of their sockets.

"Yes, Luke. You too. You're twenty-eight. By your age I had married your grandmother—God rest her soul; Sebastian, by your age we had your mother to think of. We had priorities. Goals. Motivation. Qualities you are both sorely lacking." He eyes us both, shaking his head. "If either of you expect to see any inheritance from me, then I suggest you look to the future. The fun train stops here."

Grandpa rises from his seat, nods and leaves the room. Betty clears the plates, then also leaves the room, after throwing us sympathetic glances.

Luke gets up and pours two bourbons. "He's got a point."

"What?" I shake my head and take the bourbon to numb my mind. God only knows what my brother is about to say.

"I follow you on Insta. It's all models and private jets… ten different cities and dozens of different women on your arm. You can see how it looks to the old guy."

"Luke—" I take a swig of the amber liquid, relishing in the burn as it slides down my throat. "—is that what you think, that I'm just banging my way around the world one woman at a time? I've been working my ass off. I made Stone Enterprises eight million last year!" I frown at him even though I want to throat punch him.

"Gramps knows that. He. Knows. But he also wants to go to his grave knowing we're happy and that his business is safe. He won't hand it over until he is sure it's cemented in solid gold… and right now, on paper, you don't look like a sure thing."

"On paper?" I roll my eyes. "He raised us. Stubborn old fool can't see a sure thing when he's looking it in the eye." I sip the last of the bourbon. "But you're right about one thing. If his uptight attitude means he needs assurances, then fine, I'll give him family values."

"If you're going to do something illegal, I'll have to take you in, Seb. You're not above the law." He swigs the last of his bourbon and throws me the "Stone wink" that assures me he's joking.

"You remember that girl from the bar last month? The one I abandoned you to spend the night with. Sweet as pie. Hot as hell…." And so fucking sinful between the sheets. I haven't been able to get her off my mind ever since. I ended up at the only bar in Heaven because Gramps pissed me off and I sought the oblivion that only slugging spirits can provide, then I ended up taking her home—which is something I never do. After all, you don't shit on your own doorstep. Screwing girls in my home town just gives my gramps hope that I'll settle down, and hope of great-grand-babies to a man like my gramps is very dangerous indeed—for me. She was new. Different. Cute as hell in her soft-as-a-kitten cardigan. After all the plastics and skin on display of the women I usually date, she was a refreshing change. I even surprised myself by making a special trip back the following week, but she wasn't there—again something I never do. I never go back, always move forward; that's me. It makes me wonder what's so special about her? Maybe the fact she skipped out on me the morning after? Maybe it was how natural she was. No expensive fragrances or designer handbags—just a fresh face and a killer body. No matter the attraction, I can't deny the thought of seeing her again puts an instant smile on my face. "She's exactly the woman Gramps would choose as my faithful one and only. A local girl, someone down to earth. He'll approve, that's for sure."

"Isn't she the woman that snuck out of here at the crack of dawn? Hardly sounds keen to see you again, brother," Luke says with a mother-fucking shit-eating grin.

"She was shy, that's all." She was anything but shy between the sheets. Is that why I want to see her again, is it the rush of the chase? "It's no reflection on how bad she wanted me," I reply, but it still irks that she ran out on me. We had a great night. Okay, so it's not my usual style to do second dates and perhaps she picked up on that vibe or had heard the rumours, but still, I could've made an exception for her.

"Shy? Sure she was, you keep telling yourself that. So, my bachelor big brother is finally in the market for love? Marriage? All to keep Gramps sweet so you can get your hands on Stone Enterprises?" Luke frowns as though the concept is alien.

"Who said anything about love and marriage?" I shake my head. Has he lost his fucking mind? "A girlfriend for a while will be just the assurance Gramps needs that I've settled down and changed my ways. I'm naming this: Operation My Fake Girlfriend, and I'm enlisting you to help. You can use your police skills to find her, can't you?"

"No way. You're on your own with this crazy idea. Gramps will smell it a mile off."

I ignore Luke as his hands slide into his hairline. Pleasing Gramps has always been effortless to him. "You're right. It'll need to be convincing." I walk to the bureau and grab a pen and a small sheet of note paper. I scribble *Operation My*

Fake Girlfriend as the heading and jot down what I need to do.

Find a chick who is into me (she has to be hot!) and will agree to fake date me

Stage a cute first meeting

Post a ton of dates on social media with puke-inducing photos

Show Gramps I'm interested in what's important to her

Bring her to family Sunday with Gramps

Propose—only if dating isn't enough for him?

Gramps thinks I'm a one-woman man and hands over the business.

Break up with the girl and both of us go back to our lives.

With my list complete, and with Luke showing he has little intention of helping me, I come up with another idea.

"Fine. If you won't help me, I'll get my PA onto it. She's on vacation, but I'm sure she can make an exception."

I slip my phone out of my pocket, text Rosie, and tell her to find out everything she can about Grace *Somebody*, from Heaven, East Angleford. If anyone can discover Grace's whereabouts, it's my PA.

Chapter 2
Grace

"Shit, shit, shit! Geraldine peed on Dominic's jacket again!" Willow, my new work bestie, whisper-shouts from beside me as she shuts down her sewing machine.

"Damn it. How'd he get out the bag again?" I finish off the thread on the lacey G-string I am sewing, switch off my machine, and get out of my chair to go to fetch my wayward cat before my boss Dominic sees him and fires me for bringing my feline to work again.

"Geraldine," I whisper and whistle as quietly as I can to get the cat's attention so I can quickly stuff him back into the cleverly disguised backpack, which is actually a homemade cat carrier. Geraldine's hackles raise and he takes one look at me and gives me a two fingered eye-roll. I quicken my pace, quietly begging for his cooperation and cornering him in between the coffee machine and the recycling bins.

"Geraldine, please don't be a dickhead. Come nicely and I promise it'll be fresh tuna for dinner tonight." I creep closer, bending at my knees and saying a silent prayer that Dominic returns tardy from lunch like usual. I lurch left, then quickly right. Geraldine is fast, but this isn't my first rodeo, and after some wrestling, I'm able to secure him back in the bag. Then I pull out the little package of pills from the side of the bag, push it inside a cat treat, and toss it in with him.

"How is he? And remind me why you gave your male cat a girl's name?" Willow asks as I return to my seat.

"He's improving, poor thing. The vet said he'd need antibiotics for the entire month, four times a day. Twenty-six more days and I can stop bringing him to work with me. I just hope Dominic doesn't catch me meanwhile. Is it really too much to ask for some flexibility?" The vet had been explicit in his instructions. Four times a day. Geraldine is an old cat, and as such the slightest illness could devastate his health. "I've had him since I was ten. In cat years, he's like one-hundred and something. Of course, when I got him as a tiny kitten, I didn't know he was a boy cat, so I gave him a girl's name." Poor Geraldine has been my rock through all of life's ups and downs. "He's stressed from relocating towns, and he keeps peeing on my neighbour's porch. I think it's mostly nervous urination. And of course, he's still upset my ex cheated on me with my roommate."

"Urgh. Your ex and your roommate. You should have burned the fucking house down to teach them a lesson! But, in a way, I'm glad they did what they did, because it prompted you to move to Heaven, and now I have a new bestie." She winks at me and smiles a beautiful smile with her full red lips. Willow has been amazing since I started working here, always having my back and telling me what's what. "Dominic's back from lunch." She directs her perfectly arched brows to where he sits at his desk, monitoring all the worker ants. "He is so inflexible. Since Steve left, and he's been covering for him, he's turned into a real ass. You know, since I filled out the application form for Steve's job as head of operations, I've been thinking. Things need to change around here. Where is the harm bringing your cat to work, huh? I bet Arthur Stone, the big kahuna from Stone Enterprises, wouldn't care. He seems a good guy; I mean, the Christmas bonus was awesome and paid for all of Jessica's presents. But Dominic is the pits, and if he gets Steve's job we are doomed. Like last week when Jess got the flu, he flat out refused to let me work from home. Dominic is such a douche-bag." Never one to mince her words, Willow shakes her head in disgust. She's worked here since she left school and applied for every promotion with very little luck, even though she works harder and deserves it more than anyone here. "Maybe you could try sedating the cat during the day so he stops escaping?"

I gasp. "Willow, I am not drugging my cat. It's immoral!"

"Just an idea. You're going to get your ass fired if he keeps pissing on Dominic's stuff." Willow breaks into a snigger that I can't help following.

"I should really go put his coat through one of the washing machines," I say.

"Yeah. You should." She nods mischievously. "Or, maybe not."

I giggle a snort and then switch the dial to start up my machine again.

I've worked for Stone Enterprises for six weeks now. Sewing knickers wasn't exactly the dream, but I like arts and crafts, we have the radio on loud, and so as jobs go, I quite like this one.

"Miss Harper, can you come with me, please," Dominic says formally from besides me, making me jump and jam a needle in my knuckle. He's always creeping around, looking over our shoulders so he can inspect our work.

"Is... something wrong?" I ask, slowly standing and sliding my cat bag under my desk with my toe. To my right, Willow looks on with concern.

"Follow me, please," Dominic replies, making no effort to alleviate my concerns. He turns on his heel, and I throw Willow an *Oh Shit* look before following him.

He walks down the centre line, through the factory, flanked by rows of seamstresses on either side. Then he turns left and scales the steel staircase up to the offices above. I haven't been up here since I had my interview, so now I know I'm in deep shit.

"After you." Dominic holds open the door in what can only be described as the only good deed this man has ever done, and I enter the office reserved for the CEO.

Inside the office, the walls spin and my knees tremble as the floor falls out from beneath me. "Grace, it's good to see you again. Dominic, you can go now."

OMFG.

Sebastian Stone, heir to the Stone empire, my boss's, boss's, boss—and worse than that, my hook-up from four weeks ago—stares me right in the face from his seat behind the imposing mahogany desk. Of course, when I hooked-up with him, I didn't know who he was. It was the next morning, from the east wing of his grandfather's mansion, that I figured it out. Family oil paintings of him with his brother and grandfather donned the walls like a scene from Downton Abbey. I hightailed it out of there as fast as I could when I figured it out, expecting at any moment I'd get mistaken for the help, or worse—a burglar!

Dismissed, Dominic leaves the room and Sebastian gestures for me to take a seat.

"You appear surprised to see me." He smiles, and there is no denying he is one sexy bastard. His hair is dark, tousled and ink black. It looks as soft as silk, and I remember sliding my fingers into it and gripping on for dear life as he drove me over the edge of pleasure and into a place so heavenly, I've replayed the liaison every night since.

I lower myself down into the chair and clear my throat. "I wasn't expecting to see you." I squirm in my seat, but he grins sinfully, causing my lady parts to burst into flames. He's wearing a really, really great suit, but I swear he knows my eyes are picturing him naked. I shake the thought away. He is probably here in the capacity of my boss's, boss's, boss, not my hook-up from four weeks ago. Now is not the time to eye fuck him.

"So, what do I owe the pleasure?" I ask demurely.

What do I owe the pleasure?

For fucks sake, Grace. Why don't you just tell him his pleasure is all you've been able to think about!

This is Sebastian Stone. Heir to the Stone throne and playboy extraordinaire. He's not here for my pleasure. He's found out I work here, and he knows I've been fraternising with management. Well, just him, but it's against the rules. My heart rate soars. What if he saw me chasing Geraldine?

Fuck my life. He's here to fire me.

"The pleasure is all mine." He laughs with his dazzling warm chocolate eyes, and a smirk creeps across his mouth. "Can I get you a coffee, or tea perhaps?"

"I'm not sure. Will I be staying that long?" I question, trying not to frown. Between the lust, fear, and uncertainty, a tension headache—like my ponytail is too tight—starts to pull at the edges of my hairline.

"Well, that is entirely up to you." He grins wolfishly. Perfect white teeth gleam beneath smooth soft lips, hung on a manly square jaw. I wish he'd stop; it's doing insane things to my ability to think straight and form sentences. "I have a proposition for you. Come to dinner with me tonight and we can discuss the finer details."

"Dinner?" I repeat, like an idiot who doesn't know what dinner is.

He nibbles the corner of his lip and grins as though amused. It reminds me of him nibbling my neck as I straddled him on his four-poster bed. A heat flushes through me and the room feels too warm. I need to get out of here before I say something I'll regret.

I take a deep breath to compose myself.

"That's not a good idea. You see, you're my boss. I didn't know you were Sebastian Stone when we… you know." My face flushes with the heat of a thousand flames. My hands go clammy and a bead of sweat slides down my neck. Shit. I wasn't this nervous that night at the bar, but then I had a half of a bottle of vodka down my neck and the fury of finding out my ex and my old roommate got engaged.

"I'm not your direct manager. There'd be no problem with us… spending time together," he replies seriously, then leans forward on his elbows. "Unless… It *was* good for you, wasn't it?" He frowns and his throat bobs as he swallows. "I mean, I've never had any complaints, and I thought it was, well, pretty spectacular—"

He wonders whether I enjoyed it?

It. Was. The. Hottest. Sex. Of. My. Life.

"I can't date my boss. My ex, well, he was my boss, and that didn't work out so well for me when we broke up."

"So, the evening was, satisfactory, then?" he questions, and his sexy smirk is back.

I nod and offer him a helpless smile while my face engulfs in flames.

Sebastian's eyes are sparkly and warm. "Interesting." He nods and shuffles the papers on his desk. "I could, of course, offer you a promotion. A company car perhaps, if you'd like one, with a guarantee of no redundancies for ten years? Twenty? That'd be the opposite of things not working out well, wouldn't it?"

"I've only worked here six weeks," I reply curiously. "I'm not sure that would be ethical." I'm perplexed. Suddenly, his offer of a date sounds more like a business proposal. "Thank you for the offer, but I think I've misled you. That night at the bar, that's not who I am. I was upset and a little drunk, you see. I don't hook-up. I've never done that before. I'm getting over a break up and that night I'd found out my cheating ex got engaged, and I was angry and well, you were there…"

His eyes widen. "You used me?" His sexy mouth opens, and his face flashes with a look of shock.

"Not exactly. I… Well, yes, I guess maybe I did use you a little. I'm sorry for that. So, you see, it wouldn't be fair of me to date you and possibly end up hurting you because I haven't allowed myself a proper amount of time to heal and move on from my ex."

"Hurting me?" he repeats, like I'm speaking a foreign

language that he needs to translate to find meaning. "Miss Harper, I need a girlfriend and you are an excellent candidate."

"Well, thank you. I'm not sure I've ever been a good candidate for anything before. But I'm not sure I'm ready for a relationship."

Sebastian's eyes crinkle with confusion.

"What I am proposing is that we look like a couple on paper. We stage a convincing show of how we met. We go on dates, post everything on social media, attend family occasions and then, after a period of, let's say one month, we each return to our separate lives."

"What?" I ask in disbelief. "Why?"

"Well, I fear two months would be too long. I need a temporary girlfriend for… business and political matters, and as I said before, you are an excellent candidate."

"So, you're not interested in me at all. You want to use me?" I stand, preparing to leave. I've never heard anything so ridiculous. Why would he want a fake girlfriend? And even stranger, why choose me?

"Don't go," he urges, tagging "please" on the end as though he is unused to saying it. "I will of course pay you for your time."

My eyebrows spring upwards. "I don't know where you got your opinion of me from, Sebastian, but I am not for sale. This conversation is ludicrous."

"I… Shit." He runs his hands through his thick dark hair. "Please, hear me out. You and I had chemistry; you can't deny that. You wouldn't even have to sleep with me, but if you wanted to, then I am onboard with that too. But I need a girlfriend. I'm desperate."

I narrow my eyes at him. "You're desperate? Oh well, why didn't you say so? Because of course, the only reason someone like you would be interested in someone like me were if they were desperate." I spin on my heel. Sebastian leaps out of his chair and stands in front of me.

"I didn't mean that. You're a gorgeous woman. But

you're also a level-headed, wholesome woman. Exactly the kind of woman my grandfather wants me to settle down with." The lines on Sebastian's face are deep and etched in desperation.

"Is he… Is he dying?" I ask and reach out my hand and place it on his forearm. I don't know Arthur Stone personally, but I've heard he is a much-loved member of Heaven. He employs most of the town and has never considered moving the manufacturing arm of the company to China like many textile companies have in order to save costs. Rumour has it, he cares deeply about this community.

"No. He's not dying, no more than the rest of us. But it'll make him really happy," he grimaces then adds, "and he won't hand over the company until he sees me in a relationship."

I remove my hand.

Sebastian smiles nervously.

"So, this is about money?" I shake my head. "No. I won't do it." I step around Sebastian, towards the door but he runs around me, blocking the exit.

"What about your cat?" he blurts.

"What about my cat?"

"Should you really be bringing him to work in your bag?"

I gasp. "He's sick. You can't use my sick cat against me."

"I'm sorry. You're right." His hand pulls at his hair. "I've never had to work this hard to get someone to go out with me." He chuckles and shakes his head in disbelief. "What's wrong with your cat?"

"He's old, and he has herpes." I sigh. "Poor boy will probably be a carrier of the disease for the rest of his days now."

Sebastian's lips twitch, and he lets out a faint snigger.

"It's not funny. It's a serious condition. He's on antibiotics, you know."

"I'm sorry, you're right. A geriatric cat with herpes is no laughing matter." His expression doesn't match his words at all. "So, since you don't normally hook up, I guess your cat has a better sex life than you do?"

My eyes must be bulging out of my head because my desire to knee him in his crown jewels is overwhelming.

"Move out of the way of the door," I demand.

"Wait, I'm sorry. That was uncalled for."

"Why are you even asking me, anyway? I know I'm not your usual type, I looked you up online, after that night. Surely a man of your means can just put out a request and get a thousand responses."

"You're not my usual type. That's why you're perfect. Small-town girl who likes sewing, knitting, and Sudoku. You're a grandparent's wet dream."

"How do you even know all this about me?"

He looks sheepishly at the floor. "Rosie, my PA, she did a little digging."

I gasp as pure mortification floods my veins. "You've seen my Tinder page, haven't you?"

After my break-up, I moved to Heaven for a fresh start, but it was Willow who talked me into Tinder. Mentioning my love for Sudoku and knitting were supposed to scare off the playboys and weed out the wild ones. My mind casts back to the photos she uploaded. Me in an uptight cardigan with a string of pearls around my neck. My hair in a boring bun and a make-up free face. My face floods with colour, and Sebastian doesn't even have the decency to look embarrassed for me. He just smiles a wonky, cute smile.

"You have this sexy librarian vibe going on, but I can see why you're not getting a lot of action. The "looking for Mr Forever" and wanting "six kids"… it's not going to reel in the guys, but I could help you with that. A month with me, sweetheart, and your profile is going to shoot through the roof. I might just be the most exciting thing that ever happens to you." Sebastian's nodding like what he just said wasn't even mildly offensive. Yet strangely, my body reacts with pleasure, my breathing quickens, and I'm overtly aware of my breasts heaving up and down with every gulp of oxygen I draw.

I move to barge him out of the way. To get out of this room and find some fresh air away from his heavenly, addictive scent.

"If you won't do it for me, do it for Geraldine. That weird-looking—um—cutie could use a break. I'll change the rules. You can bring her to work. I'll pay for all her treatments—"

"—*His* treatments. Geraldine is a boy."

Sebastian's lips tip up in a grin. "Only a complicated woman like you could have a male cat that identifies as female and also has a sexually transmitted disease. I appreciate it can be embarrassing for both parties, but have you had the safe sex talk with him?" My death stare shuts Sebastian up for a second and then he adds, "I sincerely apologise for assuming Geraldine's gender and for alluding that he was sexually promiscuous."

"Apology accepted. Now, let me out of here."

"I'll have maintenance build some kind of cat pen. It'll be a cat assault course with all the bells and whistles. I'll even throw in a budget for treats. It'll be a cat paradise, I promise. Please, fake date me?" he blurts with the urgency of a desperate man.

I pause from trying to push him aside and look up into his warm brown eyes. His hair is dishevelled in a sexy, just-been-fucked way that takes me straight back to the night we spent together, and my heart pounds harder in my chest. The desperate, intense look in his eyes could easily be mistaken for hunger and lust. The thought sends a thrill of desire straight to my pelvis. I'm frozen to the spot, and in this state of lunacy I consider his offer.

"It would be better for Geraldine if he didn't have to be cooped up in his carrier all day. It would also be better if a parent with a sick child had the option to work from home on occasion." I raise my brow in a challenge. If I'm going to consider this, I'll make sure as many people benefit from the arrangement as possible.

"I thought we did that, anyway." He shrugs. "Fine.

Whatever you want. So you'll do it?"

I bite my lip nervously.

"Please, Grace," he repeats. There's a gravelly tone to his voice that reminds me of him growling my name at the very moment his climax crested.

"A month?"

Sebastian nods slowly and his eyes rake up and down my body.

"I swear I'll make it the best month of your life."

A smile creeps on my face.

"No sex."

"Not if you don't want to, but I'm hoping you change your mind about that." He winks and throws me a smile so sexy I suddenly want to retract my imposing the no sex clause. "Five dates a week, a weekend away, and full Instagram coverage—my grandfather"—Sebastian looks sheepish—"he likes to stalk me on social media. Gramps' birthday is at the end of the month and you'll be invited to the party. If we've done a good enough job of convincing him we are a couple in love by then, he'll hand over the company and you'll be off the hook." Sebastian moves a step closer and arches his neck, lowering his voice. "So, you'll do it?"

I chew the side of my lip. He's over a foot taller than me, yet the vulnerability in his eyes is pulling me under.

"Okay, but you'd better take care of my cat."

He grins widely, and the action causes heat to pool in my pelvis.

"Baby, for the next month, your pussy is my top priority."

"Good." I nod, then immediately blush and his enormous, warm hand clamps over mine to shake on our deal.

Oh boy, what am I letting myself in for?

Chapter 3
Sebastian

The next day I'm in my car, wearing my workout clothes on my way to get Grace when I receive a text from her:
Sorry. Have to cancel gym date. Geraldine threw up on my Alocasia. I don't think I can leave him.

I texted Grace after our meeting so she would have my number and also to tell her our first date, or rather the tale we'll tell my gramps is that we met at the Heaven Country Club. It has a luxury gym, and I just made us both members. Running into a beautiful woman at the gym seems like a more wholesome story to tell Gramps and is preferable to, *"We hooked up at a bar because she just found her ex was engaged, and she used me for angry sex."*

I still can't believe the little librarian used me in this way. It's usually me who instigates throwaway liaisons, being on the receiving end sucks ass. Grace wanted me that night. She was hot for me. There's no way she was thinking about her ex the whole time—if at all. I couldn't believe my luck when I asked if she wanted to come back to my place and she said yes, with no hesitation, and now to discover I was a rebound fuck. Sheesh—that dents my pride and makes the centre of my chest hurt like hell. Still, hopefully by fake dating her I can get this peculiar curiosity I seem to have developed for her out of my system then get back to my normal bachelor existence, once I've secured the presidency from Gramps.

Well, if she thinks cancelling our "official" meet up will get her off the hook, she can think again.

Too bad, buttercup, I'm on my way. Take care of your pussy until I get there.

When another text springs into my inbox, I immediately smile with anticipation. I tell myself my excitement is because furthering my relationship with Grace brings me one step closer to managing the business I love, but trumping that is the thrill of seeing her gorgeous smile and heart-shaped face. I've dated a lot of women in the past, but none of them have ever held my attention outside the bedroom… or kitchen, living room, even the stairs. Case and point: My smile quickly turns to disappointment when I see the text is from Janice, a woman I used to have a casual thing with.

In Heaven this week. Let's get together?

I throw my phone down on the seat beside me, ignoring the text, and accelerate towards Grace's place. When I pull onto the street, I slow my speed and take in its charm. It's a quiet oak lined road with children riding bikes and kicking balls with complete abandon. I pull my Volvo into the drive of her bungalow, behind her ancient VW bug, and get out.

Her lawn is impeccably mown. Brightly coloured floral arrangements grace pots and hanging baskets, decorating the entire front of the property. It has a certain charm, if you like the domesticated nuclear family look—complete with the impending danger of broken windows and scratched car paintwork that comes with so many lively children in the vicinity.

"Hey, Mister, are you here to see Grace?" A freckly faced boy of about ten asks me.

"Sure am." I smile.

"Can you sneak me some of her chocolate brownies?

She said I've had enough for today, but I'm *still* hungry," he whines.

"I'll see what I can do." I wink, suddenly intrigued by home-baked brownies. If they're that good, there's no way I'm sharing them with the kid.

When Grace opens the door, my balls tighten, and my dick stands to attention. Her long, dark hair is in a cute knot on the top of her head, she has a sexy pair of geeky, black-rimmed glasses, and *all* that covers that tight little body of hers is a teeny cotton short set that shows off her shapely thighs and tight butt. Put together, the ensemble is fucking adorable and hot.

"Hi." I smile seductively. Fresh from my shower, in my workout shorts and a tight tee, I know I'm smelling good and rocking the "casual-sexy" look. Which is fan-fucking-tastic because with Grace looking this hot, our arrangement with some benefits might just turn out to be the best fucking idea I've had in a very long time.

"What are you doing here?" She squints and lifts her glasses as though checking it's really me.

"Well, I decided if you couldn't come to our date, then our date would come to you." I grin, but it doesn't have its usual effect. In fact, she looks kind of pissed off. "Is everything okay?" I check, perturbed that she doesn't seem as eager to see me as I am to see her.

"It's just Geraldine. He peed on the bath mat and now he won't eat any of his biscuits."

"He won't eat?" I try not to look too surprised. I'm not into fat-shaming, but Grace's cat is so tubby I'm worried if other people bring their cats to work, then Geraldine will eat them. "Have you offered him a donut?"

"What? I'm not feeding my cat donuts; he's at risk of Type 2 diabetes as it is." Grace ponders, pulling the full part of her lower lip between her finger and thumb. "I think it's the stress at work. He's an emotional cat, and it's bothering him."

I nod as though work stress is a real thing for a cat.

"Hmm, I see. Maybe you could teach him some yoga?" I want to chew my knuckles at the vision that evokes in my mind—Grace in yoga pants and one of those tight bra tops. Grace looks confused so I continue, "Or maybe we should reduce his workload. Help him find a better work-life balance?" Grace looks at me with disdain so I flash her my cockiest "just kidding" grin and say, "I'm pretty great with a pussy, show me the way." I make a show of cracking my neck and flexing my muscles, causing Grace to tinkle a laugh and flush all the way from the dip of her cleavage to the edge of her hairline. Seeing her smile and flush like that makes me oddly content. I caused her reaction, proving she isn't as numb to my presence as she would have me believe. The knowledge spurs me on.

Grace turns, and I follow her into the hall where it's a mishmash of pastel colours with oil paintings, knick-knacks and cat ornaments on shelves. She leads me through to an open-plan living area. Her place is quaint and a world away from my grandfather's opulent country estate... and my luxury penthouse in the city. It's cosy and matches what I know of her quirky, cute personality. I take a seat on the cushion-packed love seat Grace gestures to and almost fill it.

"Great place you have here," I say, meeting her wide brown eyes that always seem to hint at whatever mood she may be in. Today, they hold a trace of anxiety, but the way she juts her jaw also shows a quiet confidence.

"Thanks. It was an impulse buy, which isn't like me, but I guess I just fell in love at first sight." She looks away, self-consciously picking at an imaginary thread on her T-shirt. "I haven't finished decorating yet." She nods to the tins of paint stacked up on the bar of the kitchen.

"Did you make the cushions?" I ask, pulling one out from behind me. The fabric is a luxurious velvet, coloured violet, and the craftmanship is flawless.

"Yes. I sell them on eBay, Etsy, Amazon. It helps cover some pet care costs." She smiles shyly. "Why did you come today? I can't leave Geraldine when he's sick."

I put the cushion down. "I had a better idea than the gym meet-up. What if we take some snaps outside by your car? We could say I rescued you by fixing your car at the roadside. Chivalrous Sebastian, saving a beautiful damsel in distress. That'd be a romantic first meeting, wouldn't it?"

There's a strange wailing, as though an animal somewhere is getting strangled. Grace leans down and picks up her weird-looking cat. Its long hair sticks out in tufts and is a mixture of tabby and ginger. Grace smiles at it and lovingly strokes its head as she considers my proposal.

"Or, perhaps you broke down, and *I* rescued *you*?" she counters with a challenging rise to her delicately arched brow.

"Yeah, I think my idea is better."

Grace scrunches up her nose. She's probably only five feet four, and when she looks at me this way, she reminds me of a scrappy kitten. "Do you know much about fixing cars?"

I ponder her question, but apart from putting gas in, I've never had to fix anything on any of my cars.

"I thought not. Whereas my dad was a mechanic. Together we rebuilt a 1965 Ford Mustang when I was fifteen. I think it'll be more plausible if we say I saved you. Anyway, it is more accurate, and I'll let you save me next time." She winks, and it's so hot I don't argue. In her natural habitat and with her feline sidekick, Grace has grown some balls. "Modern couples, even fake ones, save each other. I'll just go get changed. You can go lift the hood of your car and I'll be right out."

She leaves the room and I do as I'm told. When she comes outside, I'm unprepared for the vision that greets me. Grace has changed into a short pair of overalls that hug her body in all the right places. Shit. She looks hot. She leads me around the car and I can't stop looking at her ass. Jesus... she will kill me, or maybe I'll kill myself since all the blood has rushed to my cock and I can't remember how to walk!

"I put on a little mascara," she informs me. "I thought it'd make me look more believable as a love interest."

"Babe, you look unbelievable all right."

"There's no need to be rude. It's you who asked me to fake it. If these pictures are going on social media for your thousands of followers, then I want thicker eyelashes."

"No. I mean... don't worry. Let's just get the shot with the hood open and I'll write the post and tag you."

She nods and I take out my phone. "Just one final touch," I say and pull her hair out of its bun so all her long, chocolate silk waves fall halfway down her back. The overall look provokes a chain reaction all the way to my loins.

"Better?" she asks.

My mouth goes too dry to talk, so I simply nod. But when she starts to remove her glasses, my hand shoots out, and I find my voice. "Leave the glasses on."

"You sure?" She frowns.

"Oh yeah."

"Okay." She shrugs. I pull out my phone, reverse the camera and take some snaps of her beautiful hands on the engine of my car, then I switch the camera setting, pull her into my arms, and take a selfie of us both with the car behind us. When I review the photo before posting it, I notice my usual facial pose is lighter, like I'm enjoying myself. In fact, I'm grinning my damned face off. No woman has ever had this effect on me. I'm always poised. A flicker of concern is lit within me that I may be biting off more than I can chew with Grace. She's hotter than any of the usual models I'm pictured with. Stunning, in fact. But I can't afford to grow attached to her. The point of this relationship is to convince my grandfather I am capable of a lasting relationship, and when he sees the chemistry we have in these photographs, he will totally buy into this relationship and finally feel confident to hand over Stone Enterprises.

"There's a gurgling sound in your radiator. You've probably got a leak in your cooling system. The sound is the air mixing with the fluid. You should get that looked at or your radiator might overheat."

Shit. I was only saying to Luke yesterday that I needed to get the Volvo looked at. Grace is a woman of hidden talents, that's for sure.

"So, I guess that's it for today." She closes the hood with one click and looks up at me. Her full and pretty lips turn down at the corners, and it makes me eager to raise them back up again.

"I think I should probably hang around a while longer since I said I was going to the country club. When I get back, I'll tell the old man that I took a woman for coffee *after* she fixed my car. That should arouse his interest enough to wonder who you are and where this is going. See, I never normally see women locally, for exactly that reason. The old man can't help but interfere."

She nods and busies herself checking the tread on my tyres. When she's satisfied they're road worthy, she stands and flips her hair back over one shoulder in an unconscious, hot-as-hell-in-July move that sends heat straight to my dick. If she keeps teasing me like this, my car won't be the only thing that's in danger of overheating.

"Will work start tomorrow on the cat haven? Dominic still hasn't announced that pets are allowed to come to work."

Great subject change, Grace. Take my mind off my dick.

I clear my throat and thrust my hands in my pockets to pull the material away from my junk. "I've arranged for maintenance to get the supplies. I've designed something self-contained. We can't have Gerry on the loose since he likes to piss everywhere, but I'm working from the factory this week, so I'll speak to Dominic. We'll keep Gerry in the staff room until we build his new palace."

Grace's smile returns, and it's so cute my own cheeks lift.

"Okay. That sounds good." She nods enthusiastically. Suddenly, I'm eager for an invitation back inside her place.

"A kid on the street asked me to get him some

brownies," I say casually.

"That'll be Rory. He's had four already today, and his mum will kill me if I keep loading him with sugar." She shakes her head, but her expression is one of affection. "Would you... um, would you like some brownies? Maybe a glass of milk?"

Yes! Thought she'd never ask.

"If it's not too much trouble," I reply with a nonchalant shrug, but I feel victorious, following Grace inside and sitting at her kitchen counter while she fills a plate with chocolate brownies as sweet as her sexy little ass.

"So, how are the rest of the dates going to work? Will I have to meet your grandfather?"

"We'll go out most evenings. I have a few ideas, but nothing concrete yet. I'll pick you up on work nights at seven. And yes, you will have to meet my grandfather, but not for a while. He'll never believe we're an item if he doesn't see you in person. I've never introduced him to a girl before, so I think he'll be excited."

She nods and bites her bottom lip, her face fills with worry. "What if he doesn't like me?"

My hand involuntarily reaches out to hers and I stroke the inside of her wrist. "He will love you. You're exactly the sort of woman my grandfather will approve of." I give her a reassuring smile, but the half-smile she returns to me is barely there. I change the subject. "Tell me about this asshole ex of yours." They say you shouldn't talk about exes on a first date, but since we aren't technically dating, I don't think this rule applies and besides, I want to know what that asshole did. Grace looks unsure whether to tell me about him. "Please, tell me."

She takes a deep breath, her full lips parting on the exhale. "So I was working for Tenmill Designs, pretty much since I left school. That's where I met Sam. Lisa was renting me a room in her house while I saved up for a place of my own. Anyway, I came home one day, and there they were, doing it on the sofa. I walked out, stayed with my sister for a few weeks, and then I saw the seamstress job posted at Stone Enterprises. I'd been following Stone for a while. Did you know they're—I mean you're—the biggest textile employer in the country? Anyway, so here I am." She shrugs.

"We are by quite a wide margin. My grandfather will enjoy you knowing facts like that. And I know Tenmill Designs. I also know of Sam Archer." And from what I've heard about him, I don't like him. He's tried stealing staff and contacts from the business before. "How long were you together? Did he fire you?" I wouldn't put it past the asshole.

"About two years. He ended up being my boss, but he didn't fire me… I… this is embarrassing, can we talk about something else?" She puts a small piece of brownie into her mouth as a distraction and follows it with a sip of milk.

"I want to hear. Tell me, why move?"

"Apart from the mortification of an affair going on right under my nose?" She flinches, and I immediately regret asking. "HR found out I took a sick day to take my cat to the vet. Which annoyed me because everyone knows the town vet isn't open on weekends, and Geraldine had piles bigger than grapes that came out of nowhere. Anyway, the lady from HR was nice about it, but she suggested it was probably best I leave before they fired me. You know, it doesn't look good on a resume, that kind of thing…." Her voice trails off before she adds. "But get this, the only person who knew I took a sick day—and encouraged me to do it—was Sam, so I think he told HR. Obviously I would never do that at Stone Enterprises." Her eyes flash to mine innocently.

"Perish the thought." I wink jovially. Something tells me that Grace isn't the type of employee to take sick days unless it is necessary. Knowing how badly she's been treated sends a flash of anger through me. Any company could overlook such a menial misdemeanour which makes me think her assumption that Sam orchestrated her leaving is right on the money. "What an asshole to treat you that way. I'll get him back for you, Grace Harper. He'll regret the day he ever let you go. In fact, should I buy out the company and sack him? It wouldn't make things right, but I would feel better knowing this was avenged."

She smiles coyly and lets out a giggle. "Thank you. I probably would like that for a day or two, but then I'd probably just feel bad. Geraldine must have had a sixth sense about the goings on because he peed in Lisa's bed the morning we left. I like to think that whenever they're together, there's always an odour of cat piss that spoils the mood. Besides, I'm getting over it, but it just hurts, you know, when people you trust go behind your back like that."

I nod, even though I don't know what that's like. No one's ever cheated on me. But I know what it's like to lose people, and that sucks.

"So, will you really help me make my profile more attractive on Tinder?"

Oh, shit. Yeah, I said something like that.

"I thought you weren't ready to date?" I ask. Because fuck no, I don't want to help her meet other men. Which is an odd thought because I've never been bothered about any of my other hook-ups moving on.

"I'm not, but by the end of a month, I think I will be. At least I hope I will be. Will you still be… um… dating, while we fake date?" Her warm brown eyes burn deep, pinning me to the spot. I had given little thought to seeing other women while we kept up the act of being in love, but with her in front of me, looking so vulnerable, disrespecting her by cheating—even if it wouldn't really be cheating—just the notion of it feels abhorrent.

"Nah. I'm not a cheater. I don't think you are either. Let's put anything else on hold during the lifetime of our agreement. You down with that?"

"Yeah. I mean, that's no problem for me. But I've seen you on Insta. A different girl every night, however will you survive?"

"Hey, don't believe everything you see online. All of those events are for business. I'm not romantically connected to any of those women."

Grace leans down and picks up Gerry, talking to him like he's an actual person. "Would Geraldine like some tuna? I bet he would, wouldn't he? Huh, you'd like that good wouldn't you, Mr Greedy Britches?"

She's so sweet and caring. Dorky, but so endearing. Spending the next month with her isn't going to be a chore at all.

Her phone rings and she answers it on the third ring. I pretend not to eavesdrop by picking out one of her paperbacks from her bookshelf, while she puts Gerry down, clamps the phone between her ear and shoulder, and mashes tuna into a feeding bowl, finally placing it on the floor for the cat to eat.

"I haven't kept it from you. I literally just met him," she says to the mystery caller. One of her friends must have seen my Instagram post.

"I am not a hussy," she says with a giggle. "No, I haven't slept with him. I only just met him." Grace immediately looks to me and blushes. I grin, enjoying watching her squirm. "Look, Willow, I'll call you back…. What, no, he's not here." Her voice breaks in a terrible attempt at a lie. "Okay, maybe he is here. I'll call you later… Shh he'll hear you… I'm not doing that… Willow, I'm putting the phone down."

By the time Grace hangs up the phone, her face is the colour of a strawberry, but twice as sweet.

"So, your friend knows about us. Will you tell her this is just temporary, or—"

"It'll be hard enough convincing your grandfather, let alone Willow. She's a bloodhound for information."

"Fair enough." I nod and return my attention to the book I've opened at a random page.

Wow.

"Grace, your book, it seems to contain rather a lot of

pornographic material?" I question, enjoying watching the colour creep up her cleavage to her face. *"Dante's length was rock hard as Ebony's hand caressed it from the base all the way to the tip. Beads of moist pleasure seeped out onto her fingers, and Ebony lifted her hand to taste his lust. His flavour tempted her and she could hold back no longer. Ebony bent to take him in her—"*

Grace snatches the book right out of my hand and holds it behind her back.

"Hey, I was reading that." I reach my arm around her waist, seeking the book.

"No, you can't have it. It's too embarrassing," she replies. Her cheeks have pinked up, and she's holding her lips in a defiant pout.

My arms reach around either side of her waist until I have a hold of the book. "It's not embarrassing at all. Your book sounds like an enthralling read. I'd really like to borrow it." I give the book a tug, but she holds on tight. She's inches from me and smells so good, sweet like strawberries and vanilla.

"Well, Mr Stone, you can't." Her breathing hitches and I know she can feel the lust growing between us.

"Okay, then I'll buy my own copy, Miss Harper. Perhaps at our next date we can have a detailed discussion of the merits of Ebony and Dante's relationship. Our very own book club." Smiling sinfully she drops the book, and it clatters to the floor. Her mouth opens and all I can see is her pretty plump pink tongue. My hands, no longer seeking the book, tighten around her waist, pulling her upwards towards me. My head lowers and my lips crash down onto hers. Her tongue wastes no time and darts into my mouth while her hands travel up and grip my hair. She tastes so fucking good, and her body, right against mine, feels just like I remember. I hoist her up and her legs grip my waist. I want her so fucking bad right now I don't care if I take her right here on her kitchen worktop. I've been hard for her ever since that first night we met, and from the way her body is gripping mine, I know she wants me too.

I squeeze Grace's butt before I perch her on the counter and slide the strap of her overalls over her shoulder. Her skin is smooth and so soft, I break our kiss so my lips can travel down her neck to the soft apex where her shoulder begins. A soft moan leaves her mouth, and it's all the encouragement I need to slide her cotton camisole down farther, revealing a pale lilac lace bra that I already know covers an absolutely perfect pair of tits. Grace's hand wonders a path straight to my dick. For a shy, bookish girl, she sure is a fox in the bedroom who knows what she wants. The thin nylon material makes no effort to hide just how hard I am for her, and a gasp leaves her mouth and sends a thrill straight to my balls.

"Mewl, mewl, bleurgh…." Gerry makes high-pitched, hissing puke sounds and Grace's attention is diverted to the cat, sat on the rug, puking.

Cock-blocking motherfucker!

"Shit! Geraldine." Grace slides off the counter and bends to pick up the cat while I adjust myself in my shorts. "Poor baby, you were sick again. The vet warned me this might happen. He should start picking up soon. If not, I've got to take him back to the vet."

"Poor thing." I give her a sympathetic smile, though my cock is feeling zero sympathy at all.

She lays the cat in its bed and takes out some cleaning supplies from under the sink.

"Can I do anything to help?" I offer.

"No. You should probably go. With our arrangement, we'll only complicate matters if we…." Grace bites down on her lip and even on her hands and knees, clearing up cat puke, she looks hot as fuck.

"Oh, yeah. I suppose you're right." I nod even though my heart's not agreeing with her.

"I'll pick you up tomorrow, then?"

"If Geraldine is well enough for me to leave him."

"Pussy must always come first," I reply, snatching up Grace's book from the floor and heading towards the door.

Operation: My Fake Girlfriend

There's no way I'll get her pussy off my mind now.

Chapter 4
Grace

I tossed and turned all night, and not just because my pussy was restless. Poor Geraldine is an empath and seems to be able to sense when I am in a panic. He spent the night oscillating from sitting on my head to clawing my toes as though they were a scratch post. Add that to my mind veering constantly to thoughts of Sebastian and I was in turmoil.

Since I gave up on sleep, I've showered, shaved my legs and bikini, and tried on every bathing suit and two-piece I own. Just what do you wear for an "accidental meet-up" at the beach with a mega-hot, super-gazillionaire who only wants you for a one-month business arrangement? Okay, so he's made it clear he'd definitely allow kissing and a lot more, but I have decided that there will be no hanky-panky. It would be immoral. If I continue on this path, I'm just a month from potential heart break. I can't go through that level of pain and humiliation again.

But. That. Kiss.

The kiss he planted on me last night was the hottest thing to come out of Heaven since Jesus himself. Like I knew he was good. I remember with vivid, ethereal clarity just how damned good he was, but still, it took me by surprise just how much I wanted to climb that man like the tree he is and rub myself all over him like a cat with a bad case of fleas—desperate to scratch the itch—okay, wrong analogy, but damn that man sets my skin on fire. Too bad he's beyond my boss. Unobtainable. Sebastian Stone hangs out with supermodels and celebrities, which is why this polka-dot bikini will never do. I yank it off and pick the black, safe one-piece back up off the floor where I discarded it earlier. No point in pretending to be something I'm not. I will never enjoy the party lifestyle when I'd much rather be home, baking brownies and ~~having hot sex with Sebastian Stone,~~ doing a challenging sudoku tournament with my friends from the Puzzle Nerd forum online.

I'm about to break into stress hives when Willow bangs on my bedroom door. "There's a shiny black Volvo outside with a super-hot Stone man looking for his date," she sings like this is funny and romantic. Like it's real, even though I already told her—in the strictest of confidence—this is a temporary, mutually beneficial arrangement.

It's not real, Grace. Get your head out of the clouds.

"Just coming," I sing back even though my heart's not in sync with my happy tone.

I fling on the one-piece and slip a floral dress over the top. I don't know why he suggested running into each other at the beach. He said it was a natural progression to the fixing his car story, like the hand of fate is at work—more like a hand of fake.

God, what am I doing? Why can't I say no to that sexy bastard?

As if to remind me of my obligations, Geraldine farts from beside me. Since sometimes his empathy runs straight to his bowels, I pick him up and carry him to the litter tray.

"Geraldine needs one of these at twelve and again at four, but I should be back to give him those." I hand Willow the bottle of pills.

She smiles sardonically. "He'll be fine. Unless he pisses in my shoes, then he'll be cat food—just kidding."

I tinkle a nervous laugh.

"So, you'll be at the beach with the hottie. Hair looks great, loving the beach waves. What are you putting on your feet? You have your phone?" she asks, listing events as though to calm my crazy.

"Yes. Thanks. Flip-flops. Yes. Shit, I'm nervous. What will we even talk about? What if I'm making a huge mistake? He thinks I'm the woman he met at the bar. The drunk version who was on a mission to be a different woman for a night."

"Hey, you'll find plenty to talk about. I've been sitting next to you for six weeks, forty hours a week, and the conversation has never been dull or lacking. Be yourself. You're a beautiful, amazing woman and if that's not enough for him, then fuck him—he's an idiot. Now go. He's waiting."

I slide my feet into my flip-flops and skip out the door, glad of Willow's pep talk and also that when I look down, my shoes are matching.

Nerves are making my heart gallop. Why did I agree to this? Oh, because I can't say no to anyone, and now that I've agreed to his terms, I can't bring myself to squelch on the deal.

A month of fake dating Sebastian Stone. Will I come out of this worse than I went in? A month of looking without touching, smelling without tasting, craving without the satisfaction of the fix. It will be as rewarding as the time I did the cabbage soup diet only to gain three pounds and have a severe case of gas.

"You could at least look pleased to see me." Sebastian grins at me through his open window. "Get in, it'll be fun."

It's easy for him to say. He dates people all the time. I have zero dating track record apart from Sam, and look how that turned out. Still, I muster up a smile and try to convince my body to calm down.

I walk to the passenger side of his car and slide onto the leather seat. Even his seats are sexy. I try not to notice his thick tanned biceps revealed by the short sleeves of his soft white T-shirt, or the woody scent of his cologne in the tight space that sends my mind reeling straight back to the night I spent with him in his bedroom. "So, where are we going?"

"I know of a great place. It's not so busy, but there's a little shop just across the street that serves ice cream and snacks if you get hungry." He grins and accelerates down the street. The drive there is fast. He handles his car like he does women, smooth and with confidence. "So, tell me how you enjoy working in textiles."

I'm grateful for his safe choice of conversation.

"I love sewing, well, any craft, really. In high school I was Miss Economics three years running." I beam. "The competition was fierce in my class but I always got it, you know?" My hand fiddles with the hem of my dress. I wish I was cooler.

"Miss Home Economics, huh?" He smiles a cheeky grin and I realise how lame I must sound.

"Are you teasing me?" I glance out of the window, feeling stupid until I feel Sebastian's hand on mine.

"Absolutely not. I've seen your work and Dominic says you are our best seamstress. You have a gift."

"Thanks. I know it's not, well, international business tycoon stuff, but I like it. I'd love to do more of my own designs one day, and I have this idea for a business... but it's probably silly." My voice trails off.

"I'm listening."

"There are other people like me, who like interior design, craft. Let's say they want the satisfaction of producing their own cushions or curtains. Maybe they want a piece of pottery, or to upcycle their dresser but don't know where to start or what colours or pattern schemes... I'd like to provide inspiration."

I peek over at Sebastian, who's thumb scrapes the rough skin of his angular jaw. "You mean like Pinterest?" I gaze out the window as we pass opulent properties, all with coastal views.

"Kind of. Like I'd have the online presence, but more like a catalogue where a person can choose the item they want, select from dozens of different materials, fabrics or designs, and then I can send them the exact package they need containing the materials or fabrics cut to exactly the correct dimensions, with detailed instructions… there could be a fan forum where members can show-off what they've made. A community of crafters interacting…." I can sense Sebastian's eyes on me, though I'm too afraid to turn and see his reaction. "It's probably silly."

"I don't think it's silly. It's a great idea. And no one is doing this?"

"Well, there are plenty of places you can pick up a knitting pattern or find out how to construct a pair of curtains, but nowhere that I can find that package, all the equipment, know-how, and materials. It'd probably fail. I mean there's probably a reason no one is doing this, right?"

As Sebastian rounds the corner and drives down the steep street to the ocean, I turn to look at him. His face is serious, brooding, like he's chewing over what I said.

Sebastian turns to face me as he slows the car. "What would be the upstart costs for something like this? How big is the market? What is the turnover of these knitting pattern companies?"

I shrug. "Quite big?"

He grins with his eyes and shakes his head. "Don't worry. We can figure that out."

Sebastian pulls the car into the empty parking space and I get out, running around the back of the car to catch up to him. He's wearing a plain white T-shirt and a pair of dark shorts that reveal his muscular, tan legs. From the boot, he grabs a towel and throws it over his broad shoulder and grabs a small cool bag.

"We'll go to that little spot over there." He points to an isolated beach where the sand is so white it looks like icing sugar.

He locks the car and I follow him across the sandy beach

to a secluded spot next to a rocky pontoon. Sebastian pulls out a blanket and lays it across the sand, ushering me to sit beside him. Then he takes out two flutes and a small bottle of champagne.

"What shall we toast to?" he asks, popping the cork and handing me a glass.

"To relationships." I smile. "May my fake one reap more rewards than my last real one."

"To our fake relationship. May it bring us greater happiness than the disappointment of reality." He winks and brings the glass to his mouth to take a sip. When he pulls the glass away, his lips are moist and my tongue dips to my own lips wondering what his taste like with the essence of champagne lingering on them.

Sebastian pulls his phone out of his pocket. "You ready for some photographs?"

My mind deliciously wanders at his suggestion, but he pulls my thoughts back to his meaning.

"We could link our arms with the champagne and take a selfie?"

"Oh, yeah. For your grandpa, sure." I finger comb my hair and wish I added more mascara before I left the house.

Sebastian scoots closer so our bodies are touching, and my lungs fill with his scent. Why must he always smell so good?

He angles the phone up high and his camera clicks three or four times before he puts it away without checking the images. Then he pulls off his shirt, leans back on his elbows, facing the ocean, and I watch as the slight breeze rustles his hair into a sexy, mussed-up style.

I casually sip the champagne feeling the blast of alcohol fizz down into my empty stomach while I admire his rocky abs and smooth skin—not so much that I give myself away as a pervert, but just enough for a thirst to develop, unquenchable by the champagne.

When he smiles at me curiously, I follow his lead, and put down my champagne flute. My dress doesn't have a sexy zip I can slide down seductively, so I grab it teasingly at the hem and pull the material upwards in what should be a tantilising reveal. The material of the dress is figure-hugging tight; it seemed like a good choice at the time. But it wasn't, and now my boob is in real danger of popping out as the fabric gets stuck on my shoulders. I smile as I tug, pulling and trying to stretch the damned material, managing to create a self-contained straight jacket with a mad woman inside. I try not to descend into panic while I wrestle and yank the material, praying it will pop over my head when I feel Sebastian's hands on mine, forcefully tugging the dress up and over my head as though I am an impotent child.

Very cool, Grace!

"Thanks."

I throw the dress onto the sand, casually smooth out my hair, and then lie on my stomach next to Sebastian, propping myself up on my elbows, facing him—which was a mistake because his eyes flash to my barely-there cleavage. Thankfully, he's too gentlemanly to mention it or allow his eyes to linger too long.

"You're welcome, any time you need your dress removed, I am your man." He smirks, his eyes lingering on the neckline of my swimsuit, gliding all the way down to my toes. I suddenly wish I'd gone with the more revealing polka-dot swimsuit. "So, where did you say your sister lived?" he asks.

Thank you for not mentioning the lame swimsuit or the fact that I can't even take off a dress without humiliating myself.

I tell Sebastian all about my sister, Florence. How she moved an hour away to work at the hospital she set her sights on, and how I miss her even though we speak most days. Then I tell him about my parents who own a car repair centre two towns over and my childhood friends who I'm still in touch with. When I'm finished and there's very little small talk left, I turn the tables.

"What about your family?"

"Not much to tell," he says, which makes me wonder if

the exact opposite is true. "Hey, shall we go get an ice cream? There's a great place up the street."

I agree and Sebastian packs up the blanket and glasses, he puts on his shirt, I slip on my dress—which behaves—and slide my feet into my flip-flops. Then I follow as he leads me to a small café set back from the beach.

"How did you find this place? It's so quiet. My closest beach is normally rammed so tight with people the sun can barely find me. Hence the pale skin." I smile, and he does too.

"My parents used to bring Luke and me here. Long time ago now. I don't really remember it, well, except the ice cream, I remember that. There are photos of us all here together. Then one day I chanced upon it, and I remember sitting in the window seat with a huge ice cream sundae. Which is ridiculous to remember the flavour of the chocolate sauce but not the look on my mother's face or my dad playing ball with us on the beach." A flash of sorrow creeps across Sebastian's face, and my hand reaches out to stroke his. Willow already told me his parents died in a car accident when he was small. It was big news in Heaven at the time.

"You can't help what sticks in your head as a kid. Take Rory. He remembers to come knock on my door for brownies every day. But do you think he can remember to take out the trash for his mother or do his homework? You probably had so many great times with your parents your brain only held onto the memory of something less ordinary. Which makes me want to taste this chocolate sauce." I lick my lips and Sebastian's eyes dart to my mouth. "I mean, chocolate is life, right?"

"Oh, it's something all right." He takes my hand and leads me to the counter where there is a small family of four in front of us. The two children, a boy and a girl, both younger than five, hop up and down and squeal their excitement, reeling off every flavour in the shop.

"You should try the banana sundae, with Belgium

chocolate sauce, chopped pistachios, a popping candy glaze, and white chocolate dipped cherries. That's the best." He stares up to the menu and a nostalgic smile reaches to his ears. "Or they do coffee, if you'd prefer. I'm buying," he says, turning and angling his head down to me.

"The sundae sounds perfect, thank you."

"Babe, that's one decision you will never regret." I laugh at his enthusiasm while the family in front of us take their order and go sit down. "Have a seat in the booth by the window. I'll bring them over when they're ready."

I do as he asks. The young family sits next to the booth at a circular table between the counter and me. The boy jumps up and down in his seat and runs around the table excitably.

"Now there is a kid who looks a bit of a handful," Sebastian whispers, eyeing the boy, and sliding the sundae across the table as he sits opposite me.

"Whereas I'm sure you were an utter delight, Sebastian Stone. Not once misbehaving in his… thirty years?" I say smugly. I've heard the stories from Willow of the eldest Stone child, a hero on the football pitch and a heartbreaker in the town. He has a reputation. "Sometimes the wild ones have the biggest hearts." I shrug.

Sebastian loads his spoon and brings it to my mouth.

"I do have my own." I point to the enormous sundae.

"Yes. But you have to get exactly the right ratios of sauce, ice cream, and toppings to fully appreciate its greatness. I'm not sure as a rookie you'll have gained that skill yet. Here, take it." He gently taps the bowl of the spoon on my lower lip, and I open my mouth and take his offerings. My eyes roll back in my head. The sauce is warm and rich, and the ice cream is the perfect blend of sweet and creamy.

"Oh my God," I say even though my mouth isn't empty yet. And just when I thought the experience was over, the popping candy explodes in my mouth, and it's pure heaven.

"Good, huh?" Sebastian asks, smiling.

If I were a cat, I'd be purring and winding myself around him, begging for more. Instead, I pick up my spoon and begin working on my ratios.

"You like kids, then?" He nudges his head to the children at the next table. The boy is now crying, and the girl is arguing with her parents because she's now decided she wants strawberry sauce, not raspberry.

"You don't? Why?"

"It's not that I don't like them. I mean, look how adorable they are." He juts his head to the boy pulling down his trousers at the table and pretending to pee. "I just never really thought about getting some."

I snort a laugh. "Getting some? Like from a catalogue?" I laugh.

Sebastian grins widely and nods his head. "I don't think I'm the settling down type. There are too many unknowns. Things can change quickly and what happens if you're not there to take care of them?" His brows rise jovially, but there's a darker edge to the way he looks at me. Like beneath the cool facade it's a genuine concern of his.

"Then you make plans for them in case. Not everything is within our control. Your parents weren't able to take you through to adulthood, but you turned out pretty great, didn't you?"

I blush, knowing I said too much.

"Well, I am pretty great." He puts down his spoon and stretches back in the booth, bending his thick, muscular arms behind his head.

"I see cocky Sebastian is back." I grin and pull my lower lip into my mouth as I savour the taste of my now all gone sundae. "Let's say you get to the grand age of one hundred, and you look back on your life. Will you be grateful you have no immediate family and a wife you shared your success and failures with…? Or will it sadden you?"

Sebastian gazes out of the window at the ocean.

"Suppose it depends if they're still with me," he replies wistfully, as though only to himself. "It'll probably be a relief to have avoided that pain. Come on, we should get going." He stands and throws a note down on the table as a tip and grabs the bag.

In the car, the direction our conversation took still bothers me, so I try a different approach to satisfy my curiosity in him.

"Have you ever had a serious relationship?"

"Have *you* ever had a serious relationship?" He throws my question back at me as he starts the car and accelerates up the hill to the road leading home.

"You know I have; I was with Sam for two years. What about you?"

"Nothing serious."

"What, never?"

His eyes don't leave the road. "Never."

"Why? Too afraid to commit because your parents died? Is that why you keep people at arm's-length?"

His hands tighten on the steering wheel and his jaw twitches. "No. I just prefer random hook-ups. They evoke less whining and questioning." His voice is hard. Sarcastic. "I keep people at arm's-length?" He lets out a mean sigh. "You skipped town because of your ex. You let everyone walk all over you. And you set up a dating page that deliberately scares off any potential contenders. I think it is you who are afraid. I know what I want, and that's being successful in business and not find myself stuck with 2.4 children wondering when my life got boring and predictable."

"Boring and predictable like me, you mean? Well, at least I'm not shallow."

"I didn't say that. But thanks for pointing out that you think I'm shallow. A useless, privileged playboy? That's what everyone else thinks about me in this Godforsaken place. Tell me, while we're using amateur psychology, why are you so needy and desperate to settle down. Did your daddy not love you enough? Did your parents love your sister more?"

The air has soured, and he looks pissed. In turn, he's pissed me off.

"No." I jut my jaw. "They loved us both, but my sister needed them more. She had leukaemia. I spent most of my childhood at the hospital visiting her. But she's here, and she's healthy now, and even if that weren't the case, I'm thankful every day to have experienced love in my life."

Sebastian pulls into my street and idles outside my house. "I'm sorry, I didn't know."

"How could you? You barely know anything about me, but still you assumed I'm so boring that your grandpa will no doubt approve of me. I guess I was just interested to see if the man differs from his profile page, but I got my answer. I won't bother you with questions again. If you want to keep people at arm's-length to protect your heart, then that is none of my business."

My hand pulls the lever to open the car door and I get out, but before I slam the door, I tell him, "At least I know my fears. I'm not afraid to be happy. Are you really happy as you are? Because I think the great and powerful Sebastian Stone is more bitter and miserable than his profile page suggests. Goodbye."

I storm towards the house as his engine roars back to life, and he speeds away.

Boring and predictable!
I'll show him boring and predictable.

Chapter 5
Sebastian

I work from the office overlooking the factory floor on Monday but struggle to concentrate. Grace hasn't replied to my text about this evening and she doesn't so much as look up at the office throughout her entire shift. When I go to the coffee machine, she walks away. And when I stop at her desk and ask her how she feels the cat haven is coming along, she just replies that it is "fine." No smile, no arguments and no fluttering her eyelashes or her skin pinking up in that delicious way it does when she gets flustered. Nothing. Not that I blame her. I was defensive as hell when she called me out on never having had a real relationship. For the first time I questioned my logic and became acutely aware that how I conduct myself is not usual. But what hurt the most was the look of disappointment on her face. Not for when I trashed her relationship with her family, although that was crass and unnecessary of me, but the way in which she threw me a look of sympathy like the loss of my parents led to my no-strings lifestyle choice. I'm fine as I am. That she even thinks a significant other is required to be happy just proves how different we are. Still, I woke up feeling like an utter bastard, and I had hoped she would be the forgetful, live and let live, type. I was wrong, and now I feel worse than ever. Even her cat, when I see it in the staffroom seems pissed off with me and hisses at me as though I am trying to poison it when I try and bribe my way into its affections with some ham. To make matters worse, I played golf with Gramps yesterday and he didn't even mention Grace, despite my Instagram posts and heavily dropped hints of a woman on the scene. Not one word, like he hadn't even stalked my Insta page.

Once the work day is done and I've freshly showered, I get in my car and head to Grace's place despite her not replying to my suggestion that I come over. I wonder how the hell to fix this mess.

I've never dated a woman long enough to need to fix a mistake. Normally, I'm clear from the outset that I have no intention of dating. But it's different with Grace. I'm actively trying to pursue a relationship with her, albeit a fake one, and the knowledge that I upset her has kept me awake all night and consumed all my thoughts. Now, I'm desperate and I'll do anything to fix things and see her smile again. I don't even feel angry anymore at her suggestion that I keep people at arms-length or am a superficial playboy. After all, I grew the playboy persona for that exact purpose.

It's this anguish that prompts a call to my best friend for advice. I hardly see Ethan these days. He moved out of town, but whenever our schedules allow we try to meet up. Thing about Ethan, that I wouldn't admit to him, is that he's better with women than I am. Well, he's got seven sisters so he knows how to interpret crazy and apologise better than I do.

"Hey, Seb, long time no see." I can hear the smile in his voice. I cut straight to the chase and explain how I fucked up.

"We were getting on so well. At the beach she chatted as though I was her new best friend, and then I got pissed because she was trying to psycho-analyse my inability to hold down a relationship, but I made a really dick comment about her family, which insulted her sister, and now we're at a stalemate and I feel like shit."

"Dude, you do have issues when it comes to relationships."

"Says you. You haven't had anything serious going on since you left town! So what do I got to do to get her back onside? She's deeper than the women I usually hook-up with, and she seems to care more if I act like a dick. I'm in unchartered territory here."

"You've got to start by making it up to her. You said some shitty stuff. Dissing her, her parents, and her sick sister. You need to understand, sisters are a sacred breed. They'll be clawing each other's eyes out over a pair of hair straighteners one minute, then join forces to tear your fucking head off the next. They're unpredictable and mean when they're backed into a corner. You got to get this chick back onside, show her you learnt from your mistakes, tell her you respect her relationship with her family and you're going to have to work to do it."

"How do I do that? She won't even talk to me."

"You got to do something to prove you've noticed shit. What does she like and what can you give her to make that thing she likes even better?"

I filter through all the information I know about Grace. While I've built up quite an arsenal of information, I realise I've barely even scratched the surface of what makes her tick. "She fucking loves her cat, even though it's a bit weird and smells a little funky." I muse, mainly to myself.

"Perfect. Jet wash the cat and stick a bow or some shit on its head. Women love that stuff," Ethan confidently says into the phone.

"Ethan, you do know cats fucking hate water? I don't think she'll thank me for drowning and scaring the shit out of her geriatric cat."

"Okay, well think of something else, something better. But you know what she'll dig more than any of that?"

"What?"

"Opening up. Try to explain why you've never had a second date. Why your dating history reads like a mixture of Vogue and the Yellow Pages."

I grimace. Avoiding talking about that crap is exactly what got me into this mess. Explaining that I don't want a relationship and never have is only going to make her think it's got something to do with her, and when I've mentioned that to women before they've become intent on changing me. Although if I were to date, Grace would be a good candidate, but still, surely it's better to avoid that subject all together.

"Hey listen, dude, I've got to go but let me know how it goes. Things have been crazy here, but when I have some free time, we can meet up in the city, okay?" Ethan is in the military. Last I heard he was back in the UK following a long stint in the Middle East. He hates coming back to our home town as much as I do. Or did. Lately the small town I was raised in doesn't seem as bad as I remembered it.

"Okay, mate. Thank you for being almost no use whatsoever." I chuckle into the phone. "See you soon."

I think back through what he said. *Make it up to her.* I said some shitty things I shouldn't have said. I upset her and I need to apologise. A thought occurs to me. A little sweetener to get me through the door and put a smile on her face. Something that'll make getting our fake relationship back on track easier for her to swallow. I take a little detour….

**

"Oh. It's you." Grace's eyes narrow from beneath her glasses as she greets me—if you can call it a greeting—then she turns on her heel and walks through to the living area, leaving her front door wide open for me to follow.

"Don't worry, I can manage all these bags on my own," I joke, heaving the four bags I have that are filled with ingredients for my mission: make my fake girlfriend happy.

I hoist the bags on the counter next to where Grace sits with her back to me, concentrating on a Sudoku puzzle while ignoring me. Geraldine looks up from his litter tray briefly to hiss at me and then continues to kick litter over his shit.

"I see Geraldine looks a bit better? A solid shit. That's got to be a good sign, yeah?"

Grace turns and looks up from her puzzle and gives me a slight, barely-there nod.

So she's still pissed with me. Great.

"So, we didn't exactly part on the best of terms on Saturday, and I know that was mostly my fault," I start. Grace stops writing but doesn't look up. "I ought to apologise. So," I clear my throat, "I've come to make it up to you. I've bought all the ingredients for—"

"You mean you're going to apologise?" she asks, turning her head and flooring me with her big, expectant brown eyes.

"Yes."

"Go on then."

"Go on then what?" I ask, confused.

"Apologise."

"I did."

"No, you said you were going to make it up to me and that you ought to apologise, but you haven't actually said it." She juts her chin like a scrappy little kitten.

"I'm sorry," I say.

"What for?" she asks and I wonder if she's enjoying watching me squirm.

"For assuming you had family issues. I was wrong. There's nothing wrong with wanting a partner and your own family."

"There is nothing wrong with wanting to be loved, you're right. Go on…."

"Um." I think back to our conversation in that car. "And I'm sorry you felt that I upset you."

"That *I felt* you upset me?"

Shit! Wrong word choices, think harder, Seb!

"That my words upset you. That's what I meant."

"Good. And that you assumed I'm boring and predictable." She scrunches up her nose.

"Hey, I never said you were boring or predictable. I don't think that."

Her eyes narrow as if trying to decide if she believes me.

"What?" I shrug. "You, Grace Harper, are not boring or predictable. If anything, you are unpredictable. It feels like every time I see you I never know which version I'm going to get. Will it be fierce, seducer Grace, or maybe timid, shy Grace? Or scrappy won't-take-no-shit Grace? You're a puzzle, that's for sure. You call me out on all my bullshit, something no woman has ever done to me before and I strangely seem to like it." She smiles a small half smile, like my comments please her more than she's prepared admit. It drives me wild with desire to put my mouth on hers. But I don't. She's made it clear our arrangement is platonic, so I follow my comment honestly, "I like all those sides to you." Her grin is wider now and I like the way it looks on her. "So, am I forgiven?"

"Okay, I forgive you. I probably shouldn't have been so probing. And I don't really think you're a shallow asshole."

"Why, thank you. You want to hug it out?" I flash my best grin and waggle my eyebrows so she can't resist.

"Don't push your luck."

"One of these days you're going to stop denying yourself, and you'll be pleased you did." *And Goddamn it, so will I.* But she doesn't give in, she just rolls her eyes in a way that says, *"Please God give me strength."* "Okay, no hug. Give me a hand unloading these bags instead. I bought the ingredients for dinner, and I also brought you a gift."

Her face lights up. "A gift, for me?" She jumps out of her chair and nudges me out of the way. If I'd known she'd get so excited over a gift I would have led with that.

She loads the groceries onto the counter at double pace until she reaches the grocery bag with her gift inside. When she removes the item and lays it carefully on the counter she lets out a squeal so high-pitched Geraldine hisses and sprints from the room.

"Oh my. It's... it's... I can't believe it!" Grace hops from one leg to the other and her grin reaches her perfectly proportioned ears. She's so happy her smile rubs off on me. Her hand reaches my bicep and she squeezes it with excitement. "It's just beautiful. Where did you even find it?"

"It's Orla Benedict."

"I know!" She hops again. Seeing her this happy makes me wonder if I can buy up every Orla fabric in her range.

"We get sent a lot of Orla's work. You know, samples and stuff." I wait in anticipation for the realisation to sink in that this "gift" didn't set me back one single dime, but Grace's smile doesn't slip so much as a millimetre.

"Thank you. It's the most beautiful fabric I've ever seen." She runs her slender fingers over the material again. "Or felt."

"What'll you make?"

"I don't know. It's so special, I don't even know if I'll be able to cut it." Grace's bottom lip sucks in between her teeth, and I find myself staring at her smiling as she pulls the fabric into her arms to smell it.

"I'm sure you'll make good use of it." I make a mental note to remember this moment. Grace gets ridiculously excited over simple gifts, which makes me wonder what else I can buy her. "I bought the ingredients for dinner; I hope you haven't eaten?"

"No. Not yet," she replies but her eyes don't move from the fabric. "It's not salmon though, is it? For some reason I've really gone off fish."

"No, I bought that for Geraldine."

"You did?" Her face lifts to mine and her eyes sparkle as much as her smile dazzles.

I nod, feeling a lump in my throat. "We're having chicken a la Sebastian."

"Sounds delicious," she replies, looking deep into my eyes. My balls tighten and my dick twitches. She looks so damn cute today in leggings that show off the curve of her butt and a yellow T-shirt that stops just shy of her navel.

"That's the plan." I busy myself searching Grace's cupboards for a chopping board. "I thought we could upload some pictures of a romantic night in. A nice meal. I bought a bottle of Chablis. I hope you like white?"

"Oh, yeah of course. Got to keep up appearances on Insta," she says with a half-smile then takes her fabric through to her bedroom while I cut up the chicken. When she returns, she asks if I need any help, which I don't, so she turns on her stereo, flipping the channel from a love song to soft rock, closes out the darkening sky by drawing the curtains, and then settles on the love seat with her puzzle.

I brown the chicken and cook the rice, frequently glancing over to Grace. Her knees are bent so she can tuck her toes under her bottom. Her frame is small, yet perfectly proportioned, and she chews the end of her pen as she ponders her puzzle. Her look is cute simplicity yet classically beautiful. Her face is flawless, heart shaped with a button nose. Full blush pink lips complete her look and her silky dark hair hangs down her back in waves.

I tear away my attention to add wine to the sauce and stir in the chicken, then search under her sink where I find some candles and turn down the lights.

"You know it's difficult to see the numbers without the light on," she huffs.

"It's more romantic this way," I reply.

"Yes. I'm sure your grandpa will appreciate the more flattering light," she says with a mocking eyeroll.

Scrappy Grace is back.

I ignore her comments since I only just got back in her good graces and because I quite enjoy the scrappy side to her character. After chopping the salmon into Geraldine's bowl, I wash my hands, then drain the rice and add the chicken and sauce to the side. I serve my dish with French beans and asparagus, then position the plates either side of her counter with the candles in the middle.

"Dinner is served, madame," I say.

Grace's pupil's flick to mine. Taking me in. Slowly she rises and inspects the food, and it's like she's trying desperately hard to keep the smile from her face when she thanks me. "I think this is the first meal a man has ever cooked for me." Her voice carries a hint of surprise. "This looks amazing."

A prideful sense of accomplishment fills me and my cheeks ache with my smile. "You know, this is the first meal I've ever cooked for a woman."

Grace nods slowly with intention. The information seemingly satisfying to her.

I top up her wine glass and then mine, and take a picture of her as she gazes thoughtfully at the food, then put my phone away. "So, how was your day?"

Grace takes a sip of her wine. "It was okay. Willow has been talking my ear off about her kid's pending dance competition."

Her eyes flick over me and she nods thoughtfully. "How was your day?"

"It was pretty terrible actually. I spent all day looking out of the office window, vying for the attention of my star worker, but she refused to even look at me."

Grace rolls her eyes and covers her smirk with the back of her hand. "What a bitch."

"Her behaviour was appalling, and Geraldine refused to even take the ham I offered; I just don't know what I have done to appal the little kitty."

"He's a very sensitive cat. Was the ham smoked? He only likes smoked."

"Dammit! Smoked ham. Why didn't I think of that?" I grin and fork a mouthful of food into my mouth, impressed at the taste. "And besides my employee and her pussy, I have my PA away from work. Rosie is on holiday and normally fields all my calls, so I am dealing with a lot of people I usually avoid." *Like my grandfather.*

"That sounds pretty annoying. This is great by the way. Where did you learn to cook?"

"We had a maid growing up. Betty tried her best to ensure that Luke and I turn into modern men. We had chores we had to do if we wanted to earn pocket money. Cooking was one such chore. She and my grandfather raised us after my parents passed away."

A sadness flashes across Grace's face. I'm used to the reactions of people when I tell them this about myself. Often people feel awkward. They don't know how to react or what to say, and I'm fine with that, used to it even, but Grace doesn't look away, she doesn't falter in her reaction at all. Instead, her hand reaches across the table, onto mine, and she says, "Betty and Arthur did a good job of raising you. You're a good person."

"I appreciate you saying that, but you don't really know me," I reply. For some reason, I want her to know I am flawed. I don't want to mislead her with the façade.

"I know enough." She nods. "How old were you when they died?"

"I was four, Luke was two. It was a car crash, they died instantly at the scene. It was a Sunday, so like every Sunday, Luke and I were at our grandfather's." Grace solemnly nods. Her big brown eyes are expressive and convey an empathy that makes it difficult for me to swallow, so I fill the quiet with more of my ramblings. "I often wonder why it didn't happen on a Monday or a Tuesday and if it did, how things could've turned out differently. Would we have all died? Maybe they'd have taken a different route, or we'd have been delayed because Luke forgot his comforter... I don't know."

"Or maybe it would've worked out exactly the same. Things don't always appear to make sense, but sometimes things work out okay despite great tragedy. I mean, look at you now. A successful business man. Someone mentioned you have a great relationship with your brother and your grandfather…." She forks more food into her mouth, passing the conversation baton.

"I guess so. My grandfather and I fight, probably because we're both similar. He's a perfectionist, and I'm always trying to make things perfect—with varying degrees of success. I suppose things could have turned out worse for Luke and me. My grandfather adores us, and Betty is like an adopted grandmother."

"Then you're loved, which makes you lucky in many ways." She raises her eyebrows as if daring me to deny it. But she's got me there, it's a fact I can't deny, even if I don't always deserve it.

"So, I was thinking. We never fully discussed your fee. The cat haven is well on the way to being finished. Contracts have been updated, working from home and up to five days, with full pay to care for family members and pets when sick. What about you? What do *you* want from this? A promotion? Twenty grand? A new car?"

"I don't want money, and it wouldn't be fair to your other employees for you to give me a promotion or car. But I do have a favour to ask, as the fake girlfriend of the heir to Stone Enterprises." Her voice wobbles as she self-consciously asks.

"Go ahead. Though I can think of other perks to our arrangement." Especially when she's looking so damned hot all the time. It's like the more I am seeing her, the hotter she is becoming. Much more of this no kissing or touching rule and it's just a matter of time before the loose cannon in my pants goes off.

"Well, it's a big ask. But I had a text from my ex today. He said he applied for Steve's old job, but that he hadn't heard back."

I shake my head. "That's not a favour."

"Well, he asked me if I'd mind putting in a word for him.

To see if you might put his resume to the top of the pile."

"Yes, I saw his resume. I already put it to the bottom of the pile. And this is the favour you want to ask for, out of all the perks you could request, this is what you are asking for?"

"Well, I'm already getting the cat haven—"

"Why would you want me to help him?"

She nibbles down on her lip. In candlelight the innocent act is sultry and sexy as hell.

"I don't. But I agreed to ask before I thought through the implications and then, well once I say I'll do something I feel compelled to do it, even if it makes me feel uncomfortable."

"Grace, this is the man who cheated on you with your roommate and then tried to have you sacked—"

"I don't know that was him—"

I raise my eyebrows and look at her sternly.

"Okay, so it probably was him. But, I don't want to be a shitty person. Like if I didn't have a job, or I wanted a new one, I'd want someone to help me."

"Yes, someone. But did Sam help you when you needed a new job?"

Grace looks down at her plate. "No, he didn't. Damn it, I'm a pushover, aren't I? Incapable of saying no to anyone." Her wide eyes lift until they settle on mine. She's right. She's sweet. Kind. Incapable of saying no to anyone. Even me.

Especially me.

Shit. I'm an asshole.

"Grace, I'm sorry. I wouldn't have asked you to be my fake girlfriend if I knew you wouldn't be able to say no. I want you to know, I'm not like your ex. It sounds like I am, but I'm not. If you want to end this agreement right now I'll walk away and I'll still keep to the arrangements for Geraldine."

"I said yes because I wanted to help you. Your gramps has a reputation for working too hard. Everyone at work loves him and they speak really highly of you too. I've been doing some digging and I think your gramps just needs to see you in the correct light to make his decision. And to be honest, Sam should never have asked me to do this for him, and I shouldn't have asked you to interview him. I'll tell Sam no. That I didn't ask you because it's inappropriate." She nods firmly as though she's satisfied herself of the correct path forward. Her reaching this conclusion makes me feel proud of her. Not that I have any right to but her ex deserves to be told where to get off—like off the end of a high-rise building.

"We need to put that ex of yours firmly in his place. He needs to know that he can't mess with you anymore." An idea that I'll return to later settles firmly in my mind. "Anyway, you're not always this timid little kitten. I seem to remember the night we met you were quite the fierce lioness." I'm unable to wipe the satisfied smile off my face at the memory of that night.

She chuckles. "I had a few drinks, and I was angry as hell. I was surfing his page, and I came across the engagement announcement… and I… I…."

"What? What did you do?" Her face is rouge; she's shut her eyes, and she looks like she might be in danger of passing out.

"I accidentally liked the post." Her hand flies to her face and her mouth turns into a hard line as she tries to stifle her embarrassment.

"You…" I'm biting my lip hard to keep from laughing, but the image is just too much and a deep chortle escapes my lips. "You committed stalking suicide? You liked your ex's engagement post. Oh no. This is too much." I chuckle and a snort leaves my mouth. I don't know when I last snorted but I can't contain my laughter. Thank God Grace joins in too or else I'd feel awful for laughing at her terrible misfortune.

"He's so self-obsessed, he probably thinks I'm happy for him. That's why he asked me to put a good word in about the job. But really, I was so angry when I saw they were engaged. Two years we were together and not so much as a sniff of a ring. It was insulting. Humiliating. So I got drunk. Really drunk. And then I saw you in the bar with your brother and you looked over at me. I figured what the hell. I hit on you, even though I've never hit on anyone, and it was easier than I thought." She's really laughing hard now. Tears are streaming down her cheeks and she looks so fucking adorable I could kiss her. "Which seemed like a really good idea at the time…."

"Wait. You thought I was easy?" I don't know whether to be offended or to pat myself on the back. "Babe, that wasn't just a good idea, it was a fan-fucking-tastic idea. Possibly your greatest idea to date." I wink.

She opens her mouth as though intending to argue and then clamps it shut. "It was a pretty good night." She shrugs nonchalantly.

I concentrate on her intently. Her face is flushed. Her hair is wild. And something about the way she makes me laugh, the way she cares about everyone, even people she has every right to hate, makes me so hard for her.

"You're a very sexy woman, Grace Harper," I say, just because it's the truth and I can't help myself.

"Thank you. You're not so bad yourself." She looks flushed as she replies. As though she's thinking of the night we met, just like I am.

We do the dishes together while the radio plays in the background and Geraldine mewls like a dying hyena. We work around each other like two synchronised swimmers, destined not to touch. The sexual tension in the air is so dense I'm drowning in it.

When the dishes are done, Grace yawns and I notice the circles beneath her eyes have darkened. I glance at the clock on the stove; it's past midnight but I'm reluctant to leave, like I might miss something while I am gone. I tell her I'm going, so she can get some sleep, and follow her to the door, hoping she'll kiss me goodnight. We linger like two teenagers who've never been kissed.

"I really enjoyed tonight," I say, inhaling her strawberry scent.

"Me too." She smiles, looking up at me through thick lashes.

I tuck a stray tendril of dark hair behind her ear. "Same time tomorrow?"

"You know where I am." She nods.

"Tomorrow, then." I bring my thumb to her lower lip and press it there while I watch her beautiful eyes widen. "I can't wait."

"Me neither," she whispers as I walk to my car.

As I speed away from her, my mind is dominated by the thought of seeing her again, and working out how I can bring that moment forward. It's also filled with thoughts of her asshole ex. How a man can treat a woman like that is beyond me. Sure I don't do relationships, but I've never cheated. And I've never used a woman, they've always got just as much from an arrangement as I have. Until Grace. She's the first woman who has asked for less than I have offered and it's unnerving.

Shit. What are you doing to me Grace, and why don't I want it to stop?

Chapter 6
Grace

Sebastian: Please wear office attire to work today.

That's it. No, thank you for last night. No, I fancy the arse off you and wanted to kiss your face off last night, but instead I put my sweet tasting thumb on your lower lip just to tease you... Nothing. Just a text that says, *please wear office attire to work today.*

What the hell does that even mean? Does he not appreciate the worn skinny jeans and sweater with the frayed hem? *No, Dipshit! He doesn't.* Why would he? He dates models. Maybe he wants me to look a little sexier since I'm his fake girlfriend. To keep up appearances.

Unless, oh crap. He said his PA was on holiday. Maybe he wants me to do his filing or some other job that I have no idea how to do?

I'm screwed.

I decide if he wants a sexy secretary, then that is what he's getting. He's seen drunk, liberated Grace, he's seen WTH are you doing here, shocked Grace, and now he's getting corporate Grace.

In my wardrobe I find the tight pencil skirt from my waitressing days, which I pair with an almost translucent red shirt with buttons so low it's almost indecent. I put on a padded push-up bra and then add some chicken fillets for extra padding, because hey, I need a little extra confidence today. I wear a pale pink lipstick because even though I'm feeling brave, I'm no good at make-up and would just end up looking like a clown in red lipstick. Then I throw on my highest black patent heels and scoop Geraldine into his carrier.

At work, I snag the best parking space next to Sebastian's car and decide this is a great omen for a good day. That's when I get the text from my sister.

Were you even going to tell me you got engaged? I had to find out on Insta! Call me when you get this message.

I stand frozen, staring at my phone. *Engaged?* I immediately log in and see the offending post. Sebastian must have taken the photograph last night. I'm seated at the counter in my candle lit kitchen with the most serene smile I've ever seen on my face.

#Engaged
#WomanOfMyDreams
#HappiestManAlive

I storm into the building, taking the stairs as quickly as I can in a tight-fitting pencil skirt and heels. Geraldine squawks at me like I've lost my mind, protesting against my angry stomp. Inside Sebastian's office, he sits calmly at his desk and I'm instantly annoyed at myself when the first thing I notice is how nice his suit looks on him. I shake off the thought and place the bag down on his desk and shriek the word, "Engaged? You made us engaged, and you didn't even tell me?"

"Grace. Good morning. Would you like a coffee?" he says, grinning seductively. His eyes move down my body, lingering on the swell of my cleavage then sliding right the way down my legs. He's undressing me with his eyes and I like it a lot more than I should. "You look sensational today."

Like a proud puppy, I stand taller. "Thank you for noticing," I try hard not to smile at the compliment and remind myself why I am angry, "but that's beside the point. Look what you did." I thrust my phone out for him to see.

"Yes. It's a gorgeous photo, don't you agree? I could use a different one if you prefer?" Even though his eyes are chocolatey warm, chills skate down my arms.

"No. That photo is nice, but you announced an engagement. You had twelve thousand likes and comments before I even knew about it. How dare you!"

He's frustratingly calm, even though I am angry and staring daggers at him.

"Calm down." He stands and walks around his desk, reaching his arm around my waist. In an almost whispering tone, he leans down into my ear and says, "I'll give you the ring this evening. You'll like it, I promise."

"That's beside the point. Who gets engaged without even asking their fiancée!" I hiss.

"We do. It was the natural progression."

I can't contain the shriek in my voice. "Natural progression? It's been five days since you came back into my life. We first set eyes on each other less than five weeks ago! What the hell were you think—"

There's a knock at the door followed by Debbie from HR entering the room. I jump apart from Sebastian as though caught behind the bike sheds with Tom from year ten. "Mr Stone. Your first interviewee is here," Debbie announces.

"Wonderful. Send him in," he tells Debbie and then turns to me. "Miss Harper, please take a seat behind the desk."

"Okay, but this isn't over. My sister is furious with me. Goodness knows what my poor mother thinks."

"I'll smooth things over with them when I see them next week." Sebastian winks and gives me a sexy smile that shows off his bright white teeth and perfect face. It's exasperating.

"What do you mean, 'when you see them'?"

There's another tap on the door and then Debbie enters the room again, only this time, Sam is standing behind her.

Shit!

I look at Sebastian with pleading eyes and he scoots his chair closer to mine, and reaches his hand under the desk to stroke my lower thigh, which is oddly calming.

Sam's wearing the charcoal suit that I bought him to attend my parents' anniversary dinner. It looks good, except he's paired it with a wide, navy and red striped tie and an off-white shirt. His shoes are brown, not a shiny tan brogue like Sebastian's are, but a matte, sludge brown with frayed laces. Seeing him again, for the first time in six months, is strange. My memories of him feel muddied by the way we parted, and I struggle to remember if he ever made my heart pound or my palms sweat. With him standing opposite me, I feel numb, like the three weeks I spent crying on my sister's sofa happened to someone else, and I have to urge myself to feel anything at all for him.

"Mr Stone, how do you do?" Sam says, rushing towards the desk and grabbing Sebastian's other hand to shake. "It's good to finally meet you. I've been a big fan of yours and Stone Enterprises for a long time." Sam continues shaking his hand until he notices Sebastian sending him a peculiar look. One that says, "okay, that's enough of the hand shaking now, weirdo."

"Is that so, I can't say the feeling has been mutual. You've worked in textiles for how many years? And yet this is the first I've heard of you. Hardly taking the textiles industry by storm, are you?"

"Um, no sir. But I've gained twelve-years' experience and I can't wait to show you everything I have planned. Should I be—"

"Mr Archer let me reacquaint you. This is Grace Harper, my newly appointed chief exec of the textiles arm of Stone Enterprises. Wouldn't it be prudent to pay attention to both members of the panel and not disrespect my colleague by ignoring her?" Sebastian frowns, and Sam squirms in his seat.

Chief exec? My mouth gapes, but Sebastian winks as if to remind me to stay cool, and so I do. He hasn't made me chief exec; he said that for Sam's benefit. I take a deep breath and sit taller.

"I'm so sorry. Yes, Grace, of course. Congratulations both of you. I saw the post on Insta and I have to say, I was shocked. I thought you'd wind up single for like forever—just you and your cat, living your happily ever after." Sam chuckles to himself, but Sebastian and I remain silent. One of Sam's many irritating habits is his inability to understand when his joke falls flat. "How is Geraldine, still pissing in everyone's shoes?" He laughs again. Sebastian narrows his eyes and I chew my lip to keep myself from splitting Sam's. With no encouragement, Sam moves onto another topic. "You look fantastic, Grace. Have you lost weight?" Sam's smile is a nervous twitch at the corner of his mouth. He's desperately trying to find the one lifeline of conversation that will save him from drowning. Unfortunately for him, he's sinking faster than a stone and I'm tempted to put my foot on his head.

Sebastian's lips press together in a hard line. He picks up his pen and scratches something down on the pad in front of him. Then, without even looking at Sam, he says, "Mr Archer we take sexual harassment very seriously here at Stone Enterprises. In the era of Me Too, I think you'd do well to remember how Grace or any other employee looks is of no concern of yours." Which is ironic since Sebastian's thumb is grazing delicious circles on my thigh beneath the desk.

Sebastian lifts his head and looks Sam square in the eyes and smiles wolfishly. "So, I see from your resume you manage 126 employees. We have 827 just at this one branch. How do you think you would cope with the increased responsibility?"

Sam sits straighter in his chair and looks relieved to get a work-based question. "I would utilise the team and delegate where necessary. I have a proven track record of managing staff, building relationships, and holding difficult conversations when necessary."

Difficult conversations? He avoided telling me about him and my roommate for an entire month, yet he had no problem telling HR about my one lowly sick day.

"I'm sure Grace can attest that I was a fair and competent manager." He grins at me pleadingly, causing me to wonder what I ever saw in this snake.

Sebastian looks to me and I stutter, "He was always very fair."

He looks disappointed in my answer as he repeats, "Always?"

"Well, mostly," I reply.

"I see. You live in Exmouth. Would you be willing to move such a distance for the post?"

"Yes, of course." Sam's nervous grin is so wide I can see the fillings in his molars.

"Really, you don't need time to think about it?" he asks. "Don't you have a significant other who wishes to be included in this decision? You don't have to answer now."

"No. Lisa and I, well, we're not that serious. I would move in a heartbeat for this position."

My anger flares. How dare he say that about Lisa. They were, after all, serious enough to get down and jiggy behind my back. Humiliation crawls across my skin like red ants. Scrap that, Lisa deserves his disloyalty. She was supposed to be my friend. She knew how hurt I'd be, and she screwed Sam, anyway. Well, screw them both! *They're both snakes!*

I cross my legs, trapping Sebastian's hand between my thighs and sit taller. "Mr Archer," I say, " if you were successful for the position, you would be beneath me in the chain of command by several levels. Do you think you could handle that?" I narrow my eyes at Sam and raise my eyebrow. I know there's no way he could stand to take orders from me. After all, he despised having a younger boss over at Tenmill. Beside me, I sense Sebastian's smile, and beneath the desk I feel his fingers rub back and forth between my thighs as if to spur me on.

"I would love to work beneath you." There's a fake smile slapped on his face that matches the dishonesty of his statement. "The salary is generous and the potential for promotion within Stone Enterprises is great. Tenmill's has a ceiling with it being so small, but here, I could really grow here."

"Yes, you could use some growth, I can see that. But could you take orders from Grace? That is her question."

Sam hesitates. "Yes."

"Okay," Sebastian leans in towards me and he whispers, "tell him to make you a coffee." His sexy scent and the closeness of his body to mine makes my heart gallop and my mind empty itself of all thoughts except Sebastian and me.

Sam impatiently clears his throat, reminding me that he is still sitting the other side of the desk.

Sebastian nods and my mouth drops open. I turn to face Sam. His eyes are probing, as though trying to communicate that I should help him. Beneath the desk, Sebastian's hand moves back and forth on my thigh. I straighten in my seat. "Okay, prove you can take orders. Make me a coffee. The pot is over there." I point to the refreshment bar, and Sam stands.

"Okay, one coffee coming up. Mr Stone, would you care for a cup?"

"No, I wouldn't," he says stoically.

As Sam turns his back, I stare pointedly at Sebastian and shake my head. *What are you playing at?* I mouth.

Sebastian's response is a jovial smirk that causes his eyes to dazzle.

Two years we were together and Sam never once made me a cup of coffee, or took the trash out, or even rubbed my neck when it was sore as heck after a traffic collision but still, I can't belittle him like this even though he probably deserves it. "Wait. Don't make me a coffee. You've shown you'll do anything for this job."

Sebastian's hand pauses on my thigh. "Excellent. Well done, Mr Archer. So that just leaves the issue of your former employer."

"W-w-what?" Sam stutters.

"I took the liberty of approaching Tenmill in request of a recommendation of sorts. But unfortunately they could not provide one. Can you clarify?"

The colour drains from Sam's face, and he wrings his hands like he does when he's about to tell a lie. "It was a misunderstanding. They thought I was stealing, but I was just borrowing some supplies. I was going to put them back. I just wanted to present them to some potential new investors. Even in my spare time I was trying to secure more sales for the company." Sam's smile is more of a grimace.

"Really?" Sebastian's thick dark brow raises a warning before his next attack. "Because it says here—" He lifts the papers. "—that the police have charged you with theft. That you were selling supplies on eBay, and that you used the funds to purchase an engagement ring."

Sam grips the chair for support.

My mouth pops open, but words won't come. *Fired. Theft. Engagement ring.* Sam had always been terrible with money; it's why we never moved in together and why I was saving twice as hard for the down payment, because I knew I couldn't rely on Sam to save his half. I thought I loved him once. I remember thinking the pain and humiliation of him cheating might never leave, like one of those awful diseases that no one can see—you look normal on the outside but on the inside it's broken. But that wasn't the case. I feel liberated. Losing Sam wasn't my fault. I wasn't the reason he cheated. That's just the person he is. A cheater, a thief, and a liar. I had a lucky escape.

"The police wouldn't listen. And my boss, he's young, and wet behind the ears. He could see I would probably overtake him one day soon, and he wanted me out. I'm sure Grace will vouch for me when I say I am an excellent employee. Someone you can trust. I'm hardworking, and if you hire me, you won't regret it."

Sam looks at me expectantly. Sebastian's eyes flick to mine, and his hand continues its encouraging strokes.

The tension has sucked the air from the room, but I know I must find the courage to speak. "I'm afraid, Sam, I cannot *vouch* for you. In my experience, you are untrustworthy and not just because of our personal relationship. You are not fair. In fact, you will and have stood on others to further your own agenda. There are no mitigating circumstances here. It would be a mistake to hire you and for you to manage the employees here, many of whom I've come to care about and respect. The problem does not lie with Tenmill, or me. It lies in you. I'm afraid you have proven yourself to be a shitty, shitty human being. Though you'll never look inwardly enough to realise this and change your personality." I frown, wondering if I was too harsh and feeling mildly sorry for him. Sam will never find true happiness because he is always in pursuit of something better.

Sam's eyes grow cold and hard and his finger lurches to point at me. "You bitch!"

Before I have any chance to respond, Sebastian is up and out of his chair and lunges at Sam, tightly gripping hold of him by the knot in his tie, pushing dangerously into his throat. He yanks Sam out of his seat and towards the door. "If you ever talk to Grace that way, or so much as go anywhere near her, I will end you. Do you understand?"

Sam nods and tries to jerk away from Sebastian's grip.

"Do. You. Understand?" Sebastian repeats, growling every syllable.

"Yes, I get it. She's all yours."

"Exactly the way I want it, now get out of my factory. I wouldn't hire you to take out the trash."

Sam stumbles as he's thrust toward the door and then rights himself. Looking back, his eyes narrow on me as he spits his parting gesture, "Looks like little Gracie finally grew some balls. I'd say good on you, but it looks like you swapped out being my doormat for Sebastian Stone's." Sam smirks.

I respond by sticking up my middle finger. "Good luck with the job hunt, loser!" I send him my evilest smirk, which isn't that evil since I do actually hope he finds another job. After all, I'll feel sorry for his poor parents if he needs to move home with them.

While Sebastian escorts Sam off the premises, I grab Geraldine, who is still in his carrier, and take him downstairs to the now finished cat haven. I'm not sitting in on any more interviews. It wouldn't be appropriate since Willow and Dominic's interviews are today for Steve's old position as head of operations. But also, I need space and some time to think. Standing up to Sam has left me on a high, though I'm pissed with Sebastian for setting this up without warning me. And the fake engagement?! That man has serious communication issues and needs to be taught a lesson!

However, even though I am annoyed, having Sebastian's hand trapped between my thighs… that's something I wouldn't mind repeating.

Grace! Please don't fall for your fake ~~boyfriend~~ fiancé.

Chapter 7
Sebastian

I'm standing at Grace's door waiting for her to answer. She knows I'm out here because I can see Geraldine through the windowpane in the door and hear Grace's phone pinging as it receives my messages.

"Grace, let me in!" I call. "I'm sorry."

And I am sorry. After the high of seeing her tell that asshat ex of hers what a loser he was and her getting her well-deserved own back on him, I was brimming with pride. That and the sight of her in a hot-as-fuck tight skirt, with the swell of her perfect ass tightly encapsulated in a fitted skirt revealing her toned legs left me reeling. I've had pretty women in my office before, but I've never appreciated the view as much as I have with Grace today. The smile didn't leave my face all day. Even after she'd left I could still smell her sweet scent and recall the way the smooth skin of her thigh felt beneath my fingers. After that I was a goner, struggling to focus on work and get the hot-as-fuck memories of Grace in my bedroom out of my head. It's like she's taken up residence in my mind and in my pants. That was until I checked into Insta and saw all the comments from Grace's family and friends on my engagement post. It obviously hurt them that they saw the news on social media.

Great news! Wish I'd heard it from you : (
Happy for you! Is your phone not working?

Who knew Grace has people that she actually see's in person. I do too, but apart from my brother, my grandpa, my PA, and best friend, I keep everyone updated online.

I should've realised Grace is not the sort of girl to save time by throwing up an announcement on social media. Hell, she still sends actual birthday cards instead of just typing out a message. I thought I'd covered the basics by texting her sister and calling her dad using the details on file at the office to tell them the good news right after I had posted the announcement. Grace's dad, Phil, seemed a great guy, even if he was obviously shocked that his little girl had gotten engaged. The poor guy was speechless, stuttering and stammering like he couldn't wrap his head around his kid getting engaged to a guy he never met. That was the moment I realised that I probably steamed ahead with my plan too quickly. I thought that if I put up an engagement post it would show her shitty ex that he was firmly in the past, and I hoped our albeit temporary partnership would make her feel more powerful and able to stand up to him once and for all. After telling me she was unable to say no to Sam's unreasonable requests, I was preoccupied with how I could protect her in the future, and getting rid of him once and for all seemed the best way. So I concocted the engagement and the interview to help her. But now I realise that I should've told Grace about my plan. Phil graciously accepted my invitation to play golf with me and gramps so he could get to know me, and I spent thirty minutes getting grilled by her mum. Now I know just how bad I messed up because when this is over, a simple relationship status change won't be enough to return Grace's life to normal. The people close to Grace will expect some kind of explanation, and it's not something I'll be able to do for her or save her from. None of her friends and family will want to hear about us splitting up from me. In their eyes, no matter what excuse we use, I'll be the bad guy. Which is the way it should be. I'm the bad guy in this story. And, with her history with her ex, people might assume she's a loser who can't keep a guy. In reality, I'm the loser who doesn't deserve a girl as great as Grace. What seemed like a good idea, making everyone think Grace had moved on from her loser ex, has actually put her in a much worse situation from where she started. Before she met me, she was better off, except from a bloody cat pen and parent-worker rights that I thought we had in place anyway.

Grace will be on her own fixing the mess I caused, and that thought makes my chest constrict and ache. Add that to the knowledge that one day some asshole will date her for real and she'll move on from me, and I feel like my chest isn't just constricted, it's being crushed from the outside in.

I've fucked up badly and set up Grace to take the fall.

"Let me in. I got carried away. I should never have posted that we were engaged. I just… things were going so well and when you told me about your ex, I wanted to get him back for you. A fake engagement seemed perfect but—" Geraldine walks right past the window, tail in the air, giving me a death stare.

I know, I know. It's not like I did this on purpose. Give me a break, Gerry.

"—I know that I should have spoken to you first. For what it's worth, I called your dad. He seems like a decent guy. We're playing golf with Gramp's on Sunday." Still no movement from Grace. She must be furious. Which I deserve. But it only makes me want to see her more. "I'll smooth this all over, you'll see. I'm not sure how yet, but I will." Geraldine turns in circles on the narrow, geometric rug in Grace's hall. He looks like he's going to— "Shit! Grace you want to come out here. I think Geraldine is about to go number two on your rug…."

Grace zooms into her hallway, whisper-shrieking at Geraldine, scooping him up and swinging the door open, not to let me in, but to throw Gerry out onto the lawn.

With Gerry safely deposited on the lawn, Grace's chin juts up at me in greeting. "You are not welcome here. Deal is off. You overstepped the mark."

Shit, she seems doubly more pissed than I thought she'd be.

As Geraldine takes care of business on the lawn, I appeal to her softer side.

"Grace, I'm so sorry. I am. I've been thinking about it all the way over here and you're right, I am an asshole. I acted without thinking, but I thought I was standing up for your honour. I thought your ex and that girl would see the engagement post and see how happy you looked—because you looked happy in that photo—and it would show them you are a million times better than them. What better way to show them you've moved on than an engagement? I fucked up and I'm sorry. I'll take the post down. I'll tell everyone you turned me down. Or I'll say you decided you wanted to take things slow. Whatever you want, I'm throwing myself at your mercy."

Grace's teeth lock onto her lower lip and her eyes flick to mine.

"You fucked up so bad."

"I know. It will never happen again."

"My sister wants to kill me."

"I'll tell her it was my fault. She can kill me instead. I'll hand her the knife."

"She mentioned strangulation."

"Kinky."

Grace snorts a laugh and punches me on the arm.

"That's my sister you're talking about."

"You're right. I'm being inappropriate. I did the wrong thing. But not for the wrong reasons. I like you. Your ex walked all over you, and I wanted him to know he couldn't get away with that shit. I'll get on my knees and pray for your forgiveness if that's what it takes."

Grace doesn't look convinced so I bend down, get on

my knees and hold up my hands in a praying motion.

"Oh, Grace, the news is true. Congratulations!" An elderly lady walking her pug calls from across the street.

"Shit! Get up," Grace whisper-shouts down to me. "Nothing to see here, Mrs McClusky." She shakes her head, scoops up a lighter-looking Geraldine and pushes me through her front door. "Get inside. And next time you want to defend my honour, try hiring a hitman instead." She winks. "Actually, don't do that. That was a joke."

"You got it, baby. I'd kill for you anytime."

Grace puckers her lips and smiles at me, flooding my veins with the sweet feeling of forgiveness. If I were to get married, not that I've even considered it before now, I'd want it to be with someone like Grace. She doesn't hold grudges and is a positive beacon in an often dark and miserable world. Spending time with her, it's addictive, and I'm not looking forward to going cold-turkey once this is all over.

Once Grace has closed the door, and we sit at her kitchen counter, she says, "I'll go along with the fake engagement so long as you pull no more surprises on me. But only because it'll look weird if we suddenly call the whole thing off; it'll look like we aren't in a serious committed relationship, and then no one will buy that this is real, least of all your grandad."

I can't help from smiling like a complete moron. "No more surprises. You got it, wifey."

Grace's face is torn between frowning and smiling when she asks, "What do you have planned for tonight's date? Can we cut straight to the photos as I really want to wash my hair?"

"Yeah, about that—" My teeth clamp together into a nervous grimace. I reach into my pocket and pull out a small box, bound by leather. "I'll need you to wear this."

I pull out the ring and take a hold of Grace's hand, sliding it up onto her finger.

Grace gasps. "It's… just wow. I mean, we could just use

a cracker ring. You didn't need to buy something so… It's the most beautiful ring I've ever seen." Her eyes are wide and glistening, but it's her smile that makes me breathless. Full and wide, she stares down at her ring finger and I'm consumed by an overwhelming desire to kiss her. Rather than push my luck, I dip my neck and kiss the top of her head.

"It was my mother's." I thrust my hands in my pocket, unsure what to follow that line with.

"I'll take good care of it." She nods and lifts her chin until her eyes rest on mine. I'm stuck to the spot, but the ticking of the clock reminds me that there is something else I need to tell her. Something that I fear will spoil the warmth of this moment.

"There's something else…," I admit, and I can't help my face from scrunching into a grimace, as if that might protect me.

"What've you done?" Her eyes narrow on me, and I wonder if she is considering strangling me for real.

"You're probably not going to like this." *She definitely won't like this.* "But in my defence, it wasn't my idea…."

Chapter 8
Grace

"Dinner with your grandfather? Now? Are you insane? Actually, don't answer that. You're freaking nuts!" I shouldn't be freaking out. I knew Sebastian expected me to meet him at some point, but I had hoped this would be later. Much later. Our agreement has taken on the momentum of a runaway train and between my growing feelings and Sebastian's impulsive actions it feels like we are about to derail.

"He wants to make things official. Welcome you to the family. He will actually be sitting at his dining table right now. Not to rush you, but we're kind of late."

Of course he wants to meet me. He thinks I'm marrying one of the heirs to his fortune.

I should have thought this arrangement through. After Sebastian flashed me that sexy grin of his, which did wicked things to my ability to think rationally, I rushed and got myself ready. So here I am now, sitting at Arthur Stone's ornate mahogany dining table that's so shiny I can see my badly in-need-of-a-wash hair shining right back at me.

"An engagement! This calls for champagne. Betty, bring out the '76 Dom." Arthur rubs his hands gleefully together.

"A celebration so soon after my ultimatum. What wonderful timing." He has a suspicious glint in his eye, which makes me wonder if Sebastian and I have been rumbled before we've even begun.

I take the seat at the dining table beside Sebastian, wishing he would rub my thigh like he did during the interview with Sam just to offer me some reassurance.

Despite the almost fifty-year age gap between Sebastian and his grandfather, there is an obvious likeness. They both have perfectly straight noses and smile lines around their eyes and mouths. They're both tall—much taller than me—and over six-foot, though I suspect Arthur was even taller in his younger years.

Arthur sits back in his chair at the dining table and presses his fingertips together. He's smiling proudly though deep in thought, quietly watching Luke ask questions while Betty tops up my glass. Opposite Arthur, Sebastian's body language is an almost mirror image—proud yet observant to his surroundings.

"Tell me how you both met," Arthur asks, and I'm grateful that Sebastian saves me from answering by reeling off his well-rehearsed story.

"A mechanic? I am impressed, young lady. Thank you for saving Sebastian, Lord knows he needs it sometimes. But is that really how you met? I'm certain I saw a young woman closely matching your description sneak out of here in the early hours of the morning not long ago." There's a smugness to Arthur's comments, but they hold no malice. He looks genuinely pleased by his grandson's revelations. I, on the other hand, feel like my skin is about to burst into flames.

Arthur knows we did it. What if he heard me screaming like an orgasmic banshee?

I busy myself with a gulp of my champagne, hoping it will put out the flames engulfing my face. The liquid is so bubbly I can feel them tickle my insides as they fizz and pop on the way down to my empty stomach.

Sebastian's cheeks lift with his sheepish smile, and he coughs to clear his throat. "Nothing escapes you, Grandfather, does it?" Sebastian smirks. "We knew each other a little before Grace helped me out of a tight spot and things have grown from there."

"Well, I think it's marvellous. What wonderful news. I always knew Sebastian would settle down once he met the right girl, and here we are." Betty's expression is gleeful as her hands clap together as if praising a child. "I've prepared a side of salmon for dinner. I hope that's okay?"

"Grace doesn't—"

I kick Sebastian under the table. Betty's being so kind that I can't bring myself to tell her that the thought of salmon turns my stomach. She seems exactly the sort of woman who would put herself out in a heartbeat and insist on cooking something entirely separate just for me, even venturing to the store if need be. "Salmon will be lovely. Thank you so much, Betty. Can I help you at all with dinner?"

Betty rises from her seat and walks toward the door. "No, my dear. I've been serving this family for thirty years and I have no plans to stop yet. There'll be some salmon left over for Geraldine. I hope he's comfortable in the drawing room."

I hope he doesn't shit on the carpet or piss in Arthur's coat pocket.

"It's very comfortable in there, I'm sure Geraldine will be just fine while we dine. Thank you for inviting us into your beautiful home. I don't normally take my cat everywhere, but he's been unwell lately and I worry about him."

Betty smiles warmly before leaving the room, and it's then that I turn my head and notice Arthur's gaze fixed on mine. There's a twinkle in his eye, as though he knows something I don't. "Young lady, you and dear Geraldine are welcome here. Never apologise for caring deeply. There is nothing finer than love and companionship. Take it from me. Reminds me of my late wife, Harriet. She had this tortoise, Turbo his name was. It used to be her mother's, and lived until it was one hundred and thirty-one. Terribly ugly thing that didn't seem to do much at all except eat lettuce and sleep. But something in that beast made her heart melt, and because of that, I couldn't help but love it too. Love is infectious, let's hope it spreads to my dear young Luke." Arthur winks at Luke, but Luke holds up his hands as though to fend off an infection.

"Not for me, old man. I'm married to the job, and it's exactly the way I like things. Though, Sebastian, I got to say, love looks good on you."

My blushes return with a vengeance. Sebastian told me on the way over here that his brother knows about his plan to fake date me.

Betty enters the room pushing a trolley loaded with serving platters and the smell of the salmon fills the room.

I swallow down a flash of bile. You'd think I'd be used to the smell of fish since it's mostly all Geraldine will eat since the Herpes took hold, but no, my physical reaction is getting worse, not better.

"Let me get you an extra-large helping," Betty says to me, loading my plate. Is food poisoning possible by scent alone? Because it feels like it's about to happen.

Once everyone has a plate loaded with fish, potatoes and asparagus, Arthur raises his glass for a toast. "To the happy couple!"

Sebastian and I smile awkwardly, Betty claps her hands, and Luke replies, "May their love be as big and all-encompassing as Sebastian's ego."

Sebastian throws his brother a menacing eye roll, which Luke returns with a wink, and we all take a sip of our champagne.

"I took the liberty of calling the Vicar. The alter in Heaven is free on June fifteenth. They had a cancellation. Isn't that fabulous?" Arthur announces.

My mouth gapes at the suggestion, so I fork some potatoes into my mouth so it's too full for me to respond.

"Not for the poor couple that called off their big day." Betty's mouth turns downward.

"Grace, it was at Heaven's alter that Harriet and I married, and Sebastian and Luke's mother and father did as well. You can be sure of a heavenly marriage if you get married in Heaven." Arthur winks at me. He seems so happy for us, holding onto the lie is becoming more difficult for me to manage.

My head spins with its inability to keep up with all the information and lies. I can't believe that I ever thought I could do this.

"My dear, you've gone pale suddenly. Can I get you some water?"

I shoot out of my seat and lurch towards the door. The smell of the salmon. The heat of the room. The friendliness of the company, and the disgusting depths of our deceit hit me all at once, and I barely make it to the bathroom before I am violently sick.

At the vanity I rinse my mouth, wash my hands and splash cold water across my face. Hives have broken out across my neck, chest and arms, leaving my skin angry and blotchy like a dot-to-dot terrorist attack—a physical reaction to my crimes.

"Hey, hey. Are you okay?" Sebastian's voice is warm and soothing as he ambles towards me. His hand reaches out to my forehead. "No fever, that's good."

I let out a sob, unable to help myself.

"It's okay. It's probably just the salmon." His arms tightly envelope me and I'm grateful for the support.

"Sebastian, I'm so sorry. I can't do this. You must say we broke up. You can take down the cat haven, I don't care. If Arthur was horrible, maybe what we're doing wouldn't feel so wrong. Just look how happy he is…."

Sebastian grips me tighter and one of his hands moves up to stroke my hair. "It's okay. I understand. I wasn't expecting him to be so exultant and accommodating. I'll take you home. I'll figure out another way to make him see."

I snivel into his shoulder. "I'm sorry. If there was another way that didn't involve lying, I would help you." I inhale Sebastian's delicious scent, committing it to memory and the icky feeling in my gut dissipates.

Sebastian lifts my chin, and his eyes settle on mine. "It's okay. You did your best, but I should never have put you in this position. For what it's worth, I've really enjoyed getting to know you." He loops a finger around one of my curls, twirling his finger all the way down to its end, then his hand reaches for the door handle. "You ready to say goodbye?"

"Yes."

No.

Chapter 9
Sebastian

Grace wipes her eyes and pinches the skin on her face, sending a flood of red to her cheeks. "Better?" she asks.

I stroke a lock of hair away from her face. "Gorgeous, even post puke." And she is. Grace hardly ever wears make-up but with her thick dark lashes and alluring wide eyes that are more tempting than the most decadent of chocolate, it's fair to say that lately, she has me mesmerised. Probably because of the sheer amount of time I am spending with her, but I can't help but feel as I get to know her soft, vulnerable side, I feel protective of her. Like she needs me even though she shows me her strong, independent side often enough to remind me that she doesn't need me.

I lead Grace out to the foyer where Luke is on the phone, and the sound of plates clattering onto the trolley echoes through the hall as Betty clears away dinner. "Where's the old man?" I ask.

Luke puts his hand to the receiver. "In the drawing room playing with the cat." He then tells whomever he is talking to on the phone that he'll call them back and returns his attention to Grace and me. "Great show you two. You even had me believing it. Tell me again why you two don't just date?"

"Because… it's none of your damn business, that's why. We're leaving. I'm taking Grace home."

Luke slips his phone into his back pocket and puts his arm on Grace's shoulder. The simple act brings out my possessive side and I'm tempted to bat him away.

"You feeling better?" he asks Grace.

"I'm fine now. I'm not sure what that was. I'm sorry I ruined dinner," Grace replies with a flush of embarrassment.

"You didn't ruin dinner. It was Betty's side of salmon. It was ruined before it hit the plate." Luke winks, and Grace lets out a tinkle of laughter.

"Ah, there you all are. I thought I could hear you all out here whispering." Gramps lingers in the doorway to the drawing room and ushers us inside.

"We weren't whispering. You're just going deaf in your old age," Luke says, smiling to me.

"You'll wonder if you're deaf when I clip you around the ear, my boy!"

Gramps has been making this threat since we were young boys but has yet to follow through on it, and boy did we push his limits and press his buttons when we were younger.

"Battery and assault are criminal offenses, old man. Don't think I won't bust your ass just because you're family."

"You just love playing that cop card, don't you, brother?"

"What can I say, I'm a hero and, as such, should be worshipped. I'm not getting nearly as much love as I deserve from this family. Grace, you're new to town, so I'll give you a break since you probably haven't heard about me yet. But you appreciate a hard-working cop, don't you?"

Grace's teeth pinch the corner of her lips in a smile. "Oh, I've heard about you, all right."

"What does that mean?" I ask curiously. No way, she's

into my brother like the rest of the women are in this town. Luke's known as the *heartbreak cop,* but surely Grace isn't affected by his charms.

"Do I detect jealousy, brother?" Luke looks pleased with himself, and so I dig him discreetly in the ribs. "So, Grace, what have you heard? You know it's all true." He makes a ludicrous size gesture using both hands, then adds, "Well, the good stuff is. Tell me it's all good that you've heard?"

Before she has a chance to answer, I inform Gramps that we're going.

""You don't mind if I steal Sebastian away for a little while first, do you Grace? I'm working nights the rest of this week and there's something I need to talk to my big brother about."

"Yes, I mind. We're leaving now," I reply at the same time Grace says, "That'd be okay, I don't mind waiting."

"Are you sure you don't mind? Thank you." Luke throws me a shit-eating grin and ushers me to the door. Suddenly I feel apprehensive about leaving Grace in this room with my grandfather. Not that he'd be rude or unkind, he's an all-around great guy. But it's exactly the kind of situation that will cause Grace stress.

"You boys go. Give me a chance to get to know my future granddaughter-in-law. Besides, Betty will be through in a moment with Geraldine's supper. If you're well enough to hang with me while the boys probably embark on yet another urination contest?"

"It'd be my pleasure to hang with you, Arthur." Grace smiles politely, and so I allow Luke to drag me from the room by my arm.

"I'll be right back. Ten minutes tops," I promise Grace.

"Okay." She smiles sweetly and my grandfather ushers her to the leather chairs by the window.

Shit. I hope she's not about to get the Spanish Inquisition.

**

"So, why did you pull me away from my girlfriend? What's so important?" I ask as Luke hands me a snooker cue.

"*Girlfriend?*" Luke raises his eyebrows.

I roll my eyes at his cocky stance. "You know what I mean."

"I just wanted to check on how this crazy plan of yours is coming along. Can't a brother check in on his brother?" There's a crack in the air as Luke leans down over the pool table to break the balls. "Besides, Grace will be okay with Gramps, she's practically family now, after all."

I take my shot and think about how to phrase my update. "About that. I'm sorry I didn't tell you about the engagement. To be fair, I didn't tell Grace either. I just got swept away in the—"

"You didn't tell Grace?" Luke lets out a howling laugh and shakes his head. "How the fuck did you get engaged without telling your fiancée?"

"That's a good question. Her ex is an asshole, and Grace and I were getting on so well. She's different. I can't explain it. Like she gets me. Or rather, she doesn't let me get away with shit. She's honest with me, despite who I am and my reputation. It's refreshing. And I get her, and she's got these huge expressive eyes that just pull me in and before I know it I'm spilling all my shit—"

Luke sits on one of the high-backed, winged chairs facing the pool table. "You're in love with her, aren't you?" If Luke was shocked at the news of our engagement, he's positively floored now.

"No." I shake my head. "Don't be absurd. There's one reason I'm spending time with Grace, and that's convincing the old man I've changed. I'm not…" Even as I'm explaining, in the back of my mind, I know when I drop Grace off home tonight it won't be the last time I see her. I'd planned on investing in her home craft business, if she'd let me. We'd need to spend time together to get the idea up and running. And then there's Geraldine's health. I'm sticking to my end of the bargain, even though things didn't turn out the way I planned, and I want to see the return on my investment. If his health doesn't improve, then I was planning on finding a geriatric cat specialist.

"You're thinking about her, aren't you? Your face has gone all weird and dreamy, and you're fucking smiling like a love sick puppy."

"I am not smiling like anything. She's fucking hot. I'd have to be gay, blind, or an idiot not to have the hots for her."

"She is pretty hot. I wouldn't normally be inclined to hop on your seconds, but for Grace I think I'd make an exception. Tell me, is she—" I'm across the room and have my hand wrapped around Luke's throat before he's finished his sentence. "Kidding, man. Just. Kidding." I loosen my grip then let go, stepping aside. "You've got it bad. I've never seen you like this."

"She's fucking exceptional." I drag my hands through my hair. I know Luke would never pick up where I left off with Grace, it's our one cardinal rule that neither of us will ever break. "Every day I spend with her just leaves me wanting more. Besides, she wouldn't look twice at you. She's hot for me. That night we hooked up, we were fucking on fire, it was so hot. She agreed to do all this for me." I hold my hands up. "Since all she's got out of our arrangement is a cat den at work and some employee benefits for her friend, it's obvious she's hot for me, or else why would she agree?"

"So she's done all this because she's hot in love with you? Nah, I don't buy it. You ain't all that. You must be paying her." Luke winks and I shake my head at him. Grace isn't materialistic or money grabbing, she's the most genuinely kind person I've met in a very long time.

My attention is pulled away from my thoughts by a light cough over near the doorway.

"Grace, we were just about to come check on you. Hope Gramps hasn't been too inquisitive." Luke fills the silence while I freak out over how much of our conversation she just heard, and how the hell I'm going to fix it if she did hear.

"He's been very... courteous. He wants you both in the drawing room when you've finished."

Grace stomps from the room before I have a chance to ask her how she is or follow.

"Man, she looks pissed with you. Wouldn't want to be in your shoes when she gets you on your own."

I open my mouth, intending to argue and blame him for insinuating she is in this for money, but there's no point. Luke didn't mean any harm. So I clamp my mouth shut. Grace *did* look pissed. Which means she either heard Luke and I discuss whether she had entered into our agreement for love or money, or my grandfather said something to rile her. I fear it's the latter.

"Come on, let's go."

I pause at the door to the drawing room and watch Grace laughing at something my grandfather has said. She and Gramps are seated by the window. Gramps has Geraldine on his lap while Grace has one of the family photo albums on hers.

"There you two are. Finally. I was just telling Grace what a curious, effervescent young man you were, Sebastian."

Since that does not sound good, I wonder closer.

"Shit, why are you showing her that?!" I snatch the album off Grace's lap and hold it behind my back, but I know it's too late; she's seen the toddler pic of me attempting to pull my genitals into my mouth. "I've grown quite a bit since then. As a person, and as a man...." I babble like an idiot.

"Oh, I think she knows just how much you've grown... as a person." Luke snorts with laughter.

"Now, now, Sebastian. You were a healthy, inquiring child. I was actually showing her your mother and father's wedding photos right before that, when this photograph just appeared as if out of nowhere." Gramps covers his laugh with a cough. "But that's not the reason I called you in. Young Grace has just been telling me all about her interior craft business, and I for one think it's a wonderful idea. I'm going to invest. Mathew will draw up some preliminary agreements, but I thought it would be good for you to work with your future wife on this—take care of my investment, as it were. I'm too old to start a new venture."

"That's what I've been trying to tell you, old man." I flash my brows in an "I told you so" gesture that is lost on my grandfather. Grace doesn't even make eye contact. "There's no need for you to invest. I already decided to invest in Grace's company."

"Oh, did you, Sebastian? Only I don't remember you asking. Whereas Arthur has asked all sorts of questions, while you've been *chatting* to your brother. So, maybe I'd rather work with Arthur on this, if you don't mind." A satisfied, pissed grin flashes across Grace's face and her eyes momentarily flash to mine before returning to Gramps'.

"Good." Gramps' hands rub together and then he returns them to scratch behind Geraldine's ear. "I'm glad that's settled. I'll have Mathew call you once you've finalised your business plan. Can you have it ready by the first of next month? That gives you two weeks." Grace nods as if in a daze and Gramps shakes her hand. She thanks him for a lovely evening, but something in the paleness of her usually tan skin and her confused expression worries me. I hand Grace the cat bag, which she grabs carefully, avoiding my touch. Gramps hands her Gerry and they fuss over him for a while before she scoops him into the carrier. Meanwhile, I'm left neglected and out in the cold.

Once the goodbyes are said and Grace has promised to return soon, she walks ahead of me, putting the cat bag onto the back seat of the Volvo, and then she slides into the passenger seat.

Gramps claps me on the back from the staircase to the main entrance of his country manor. "You've done well, my dear Sebastian. She's quite a catch. I like her."

"She is incredible," I reply, momentarily unsettled how quickly my words surfaced and how heartfelt they are. My grandfather's eyes brim with pride. "Which makes me wonder why you, old man, are trying to scare her off with my childhood dick pics?" I glare at him. He may act an old fool at times, but Arthur Stone's actions are always guided by judgement rather than chance.

Gramps chuckles deeply and wraps an arm over my shoulder. "Grace was keen to hear all about you. I filtered the things she may want to hear from you herself, but she is wildly keen on you, that much is obvious. I haven't had anyone to share the good stuff in such a long time. I think I'm going to enjoy seeing the family expand." Gramps laughs again. "Such a wild child you were. If I told you you'd fall from the old oak tree, you'd just climb higher to prove me wrong. It's refreshing to watch someone prove you wrong for once."

"Prove me wrong? I'm never wrong." I roll my eyes.

Gramps laughs and winks one of his already crinkled eyes. "I used to think that way too. And you used to think love wasn't for you. Now that you have the love of a good woman, you'll find you're wrong at least as often as you are right. But that's okay, commitment won't work without compromise. Now, off you go. Don't keep the lady waiting."

I walk down the steps away from Gramps, wondering how I feel about his assumption that Grace is in love with me. He can't surely know that just from tonight? I mean, I know she likes me, but love… that's a wholly different concept altogether.

Grace is quiet the entire length of Gramps' driveway. Her place is only ten minutes away, but for five minutes the tension hanging in the air is so thick I have to break the silence or risk drowning.

"So, you want my grandfather to invest in your business?" I ask, still pissed she chose him over me.

"He seemed really interested in the concept. Apparently he has fingers in similar pies," she replies indifferently.

"He does. In the seventies and eighties Stone Enterprises cornered the worldwide market on pattern production. Sewing your own clothes and that kind of thing, but I did some research, and the market is definitely growing again."

Grace doesn't respond. She's looking out of the window and without being able to see her face, it's difficult to know just how pissed she is with me.

"I was going to offer to invest. I'd planned to talk to you about it tonight."

Her head suddenly spins in my direction. "You were going to talk to me about it tonight? That's awfully good of you, Sebastian." She barks my name like it's an insult. "Because, talking *to* me, instead of *about* me, is definitely preferable!"

At Grace's place, I pull in and switch off the engine.

"Shit," I whisper under my breath. "How much did you hear?"

"Enough to be pissed off with you—*again*. You think I helped you because I'm some pushover harpy that's in love with you? Do you even realise how pathetic that makes me feel? I offered to help you because it's who I am. I help people if I can. I open doors for people. I give lifts even when I'm not going that way, and I get Mrs McClusky's shopping while I'm getting my own and sometimes even when I'm not. I don't want to live in a world where people don't give a shit. But the way you spoke about me to your brother, you made me feel weak, like I was stupid not to see you were taking advantage of me."

It's dark outside. The only light filtering into the car is from the streetlight outside. It throws just enough light onto Grace's face to highlight her glistening eyes, and a lump as thick and prickly as a cactus takes root in my throat.

Grace's hand reaches for the door handle. "I guess this is goodbye. Tell Arthur, I appreciate his generous offer but with you and I no longer together, it would be a mistake to enter into a partnership." Grace slides out of the passenger seat and clicks the door shut behind her. She opens the rear door and collects Geraldine. My chest constricts, crushing my heart as I watch her walk out of my life.

Chapter 10
Grace

Keys. Damn it. Keys, where are you?

Eyes, stop leaking. You have no business leaking.

Sebastian's words replay in my mind. *She wouldn't look twice at you. She's hot for me. That night we hooked-up, we were fucking on fire, it was so hot. She agreed to do all this for me. Since all she's got out of this is a cat den at work and some employee benefits for her friend, it's clear she's got to be hot for me or else why would she agree?*

I've been so stupid. I feel so used. Which is ridiculous because I willingly agreed to fake date Sebastian. I knew I found him attractive, and I knew exactly how he made me feel in the bedroom. And I also knew, if I'm honest with myself, that spending time with him would be my undoing.

If I can just get myself inside without breaking down. If I can just hold myself together until Sebastian's car pulls away, then maybe I can put everything in perspective and my emotions won't feel as raw as they do right now.

I know I put the keys in this pocket, right here, somewhere. My hand is blindly searching and Geraldine is mewling like he was the one who had his heart broken tonight. Which is crazy because he doesn't even like

Sebastian. Okay, so maybe he does a little, but I definitely don't. Not anymore.

Bingo. My hands find the smooth edge of my flashlight keyring and I pull them out of my bag and fumble for the lock.

"Wait." Sebastian's voice is smooth and inviting behind me. I don't turn around. How can I when pathetic tears threaten to spill from my eyes?

"Go away." I wrestle with the lock and push on the door the second there is movement. Then I take one step inside and lower Geraldine, still in his carrier, inside the door. Sebastian's hand grabs the edge of the door above mine before I get the chance to slip inside—securing it somewhere between open and closed.

"You said I thought you were pathetic. You've got this all wrong."

I don't turn around and face him. "It's fine. I can see why you might think that. Please go." Sebastian's body is close behind mine. So close I can smell his heavenly scent and feel the heat radiating from him.

"I don't think that. You heard me all wrong. At least, without hearing everything I said, it's out of context. Luke asked me if I was falling for you. I didn't know what to say." His voice is low and gravelly. My stomach clenches with ardent yearning. "I only know that since I met you, I've used every excuse I could find to spend more time with you. Like I can't get enough. I'm not used to feeling this way. I've never felt this way about a woman. I told Luke that I hoped you felt like this about me. But I don't know. I don't fucking know how you feel and that scares the shit out of me." His hand moves from holding the door, to holding my hand. He uses this as leverage to turn me to face him. When I dare to meet his gaze, the intensity of his eyes makes my heart skip a beat. "I don't think you're weak. You're sweet and kind, but you're also strong. You don't always speak your mind, but you're not afraid to, and when you do, your words are filled with dignity and grace, and a quiet confidence. I'm out on a limb and have no control over this situation, but I don't want the last time I see you to be you walking away from me tonight."

Sebastian towers above me. A foot taller than me and so close our chests are almost touching. In the low light, his eyes look almost entirely black and ringed with dark circles, throwing an almost haunted look across his face. I close my mouth to swallow my surprise, but my mind is emptied as my eyes are drawn to his mouth. Lips that are soft and inviting, speaking the words that I sought but were afraid to hear and as if pulled by magnets, I lift myself onto my toes and reach up to skim my lips against his. As soon as our mouths connect, my eyes flutter closed and instinct takes over.

Sebastian's hands cup my chin, gently at first, boosting what begins as an innocent connection into a unifying bond. Unsatisfied with his loose hold on me, his hands reach up and fist my hair, holding me in place while his tongue savagely dips into my mouth. My own hands, empty of the leverage they need to stop me from falling, grip his hips. As the intensity of our kiss deepens, so does my desperation to feel more of him. The inside of my thighs throb for his touch, like the sexual tension has been mounting since our first encounter and I can't wait a moment longer for its release. I thought he saw me as weak. A pushover. Just like Sam did. His confession, honest and raw, that he wants me too and not just in his bed, and that he is as consumed by me as I am him breaks down the last of my defences. I'm powerless to stop from falling into him and most importantly, I don't want to stop. Suddenly each and every exchange between us, the lingering looks and thoughtful smiles, every conversation and comment, it feels like it has been building up to this moment. I need more of him. Without conscious thought, I untuck his shirt and my hands glide across the smooth skin of his abs, all the way around to the hard muscles of his back. Sebastian lets out a soft moan in my mouth, and heat floods my vagina. It's all the signal I need to unleash my desire and make this happen. I need him inside me right now and I'm done waiting.

I fist his shirt, pulling him inside my hallway and kicking the front door shut with my foot. Geraldine hisses, reminding me he is still in his carrier on the floor, but not even his cranky temperament can lure me into stopping now. Sure, he'll be pissed off with being stuck in the hallway, but right now, I'm guided by one pussy alone—my own.

We kiss down the length of the hall and I pull Sebastian by his shirt towards my bedroom and kick open the door, breaking our kiss to kick off my shoes and walking backwards until I'm perching on the comforter of my bed.

"Fuck. You are so beautiful," he growls, pulling off his shoes and socks in one swift move and slowly walking towards me.

Anticipation has my nerves zinging within me. I draw my lower lip into my mouth and suck it to contain my excitement.

Once he is standing before me and looking searchingly into my eyes he says, "Are you sure?"

I part my thighs and pull him closer by his belt buckle. "Yes."

His head dips down and his velvety lips take mine. Softly at first but quickly building to fervent as we are gripped by need. Sebastian's hands reach down to the hem of my shirt, and he breaks our kiss to pull it over my head. His eyes dip down to my breasts and he licks his lips, then pushes me back on the bed so he can pull away my jeans. I scoot farther back on the bed and when Sebastian joins me he is sans clothes, apart from his boxers. My mouth falls open. Sebastian naked and on my bed next to me is like having everything I ever wanted for Christmas but forgot to ask for. Rock hard abs? Check. Smooth tanned skin? Check. Strong, muscular biceps? Check. A cute, tight ass that I want to pinch so hard I leave nail prints? Check.

He smiles seductively. "What?"

"Nothing. It's just you're naked. Here, right next to me."

I breathe out a happy sigh.

"Baby, there's no place in the world I'd swap for right here." His eyes flick across my body and his hand reaches down and grips my ankle. He smooths his hand all the way up my leg until it pauses on the hem of my panties. "I'm going to make you feel so good."

My heart triples its beat at his promise. His eyes linger on mine while his finger strokes beneath the hem to caress my wetness, and then his lips crash down on mine. My hand moves to slide his boxers over his hips and he makes quick work of pulling them off, then, with my eyes on the prize, I find his enormous and smooth, velvety length. He feels so good filling my palm.

His touch quickly returns to exactly where I need it, a gentle warning at first, builds into a powerful rhythmic torment. Bringing me close, then backing away until I am begging him to give me what I need. My eyes flicker open and close on the brink of ecstasy. Pre-cum has lubricated his length and my hand slides up and down with ease, working him into a frenzy too until the pleasure becomes too much and I have no choice but to release him so I can cling onto his shoulders as pulses of pleasure explode within me like fireworks on the fourth of July. I ride the waves of pleasure, losing sense of time and place. All that anchors me to this world is clinging to Sebastian's shoulders and breathing in his rugged, woody scent. When I open my eyes, I see Sebastian watching me as though mesmerized by my actions while sporting a fiercely heated gaze.

"I want to watch you come for me every day. Every day. I'm going to rock up here, do that and watch you explode. Hottest. Thing. I. Ever. Saw."

His pillow talk makes me giggle until his eyes darken again and he pulls away my bra. When Sebastian takes the bud of my breast in his mouth and swirls his tongue, I let out a hiss and grip his shoulder.

"Fuck. I need you," he growls and his arms snake around me, pulling me closer. Chest to chest. Skin to skin. My nerves are on fire.

"I need you too," I whisper breathlessly.

He kisses me deeply, then lets go of me to get down from the bed. He lifts his jeans from the floor and searches in his pockets for his wallet. He is quickly sheathed and lowering himself on me moments later.

"You're beautiful." His eyes are ablaze with desire and it makes me feel both beautiful and powerful. I lean up and pull his lower lip into my mouth, arching my back to bring my pelvis closer to the promised land. Sebastian's breathing hitches as he enters me achingly slowly, and his eyes clench as he lets out a guttural moan. He fills me, pausing once until he is balls deep, allowing me time to adjust to his presence. Sebastian's shoulders are thick and muscular, just right for clinging onto while I allow him to take the lead. His rhythm starts slow but speeds to a crescendo of pleasure. His body is perfectly sculpted, and he knows how to use it. A delicious friction builds in my pelvis, and even though my nails are digging into his shoulders, I am powerless to unclench my grip.

My breathing is a mess—all ragged breaths and whispered pleas. Our bodies are coated in a sheen of perspiration, and I cling to him, calling out his name and driving the fingers of my right hand into his hair, pulling him down to kiss me as my pleasure reaches the point of no return. His pace quickens, and I teeter on the edge of oblivion momentarily until my body starts to judder and rock with the delicious pleasure bomb detonated within me. Sebastian grips my hair and kisses me harder, growling my name into my mouth. My hands move to squeeze the tight muscles of his ass, and I relish in the sensation of his final shudders as we cling to each other, riding the aftershocks.

When our breathing returns to normal, Sebastian pulls us onto our sides, facing each other. My head is resting on a pillow, and I'm satiated and in a blissful state. Sebastian's ruggedly handsome face is right in front of me, and I'm about to reach out and stroke the smooth line of his jaw when Sebastian beats me to it. His index finger reaches out and gently swipes across my lower lip, trailing a path down to my collar bone, across my breast, all the way to my hip where he lazily draws circles with his fingers on my skin.

"You have the softest skin. More exquisite than the finest silk. Tastier than the finest food." His eyes flick up to mine. "Your perfection constantly surprises me, Grace Harper."

My brow raises in languid interest. "Perfection? I'm far from perfect." I laugh and brush off the compliment. No one has ever told me that I am perfect, and now the grin won't leave my face. "Were you expecting something less satisfactory?" I goad.

"I already knew we fit together perfectly in the bedroom. But, I don't know..." Sebastian lies back and stares at the ceiling. "I don't suppose I was expecting anything. Certainly not this." His arm pulls me closer so my head rests on his shoulder and he kisses the top of my head. He's quiet for a while, and I wonder what happens now. Will Sebastian get dressed, thank me for a good time and leave? Sleeping together doesn't guarantee a happy ever after. He must have been having similar thoughts because he idly suggests, "What if we were to actually date. Just to see where this thing between us goes. No pressure. No expectations. Just two people who happen to be extraordinarily attracted to one another letting the chips fall...."

His voice trails off, and I lay blissfully running my fingers over his smooth chest and across the divots of his abdomen. "I like that idea." I take a fleeting look up at Sebastian's face. He's smiling down at me, his fingers twirling through my hair. "But you forgot about the engagement." I hold my ring finger, weighed down by a huge diamond in the air. "It adds a certain amount of pressure and expectations, don't you think?"

"I think we should leave the ring where it is for now, and not because my grandfather likes it there, but because I like seeing you wear it."

"Maybe leaving it where it is will just make me wonder if this is all still fake. If now you are playing me and your grandfather."

"If that's what you are worrying about, then I haven't made my feelings clear enough and therefore must reiterate them." Sebastian pulls me up into a long, lingering kiss. "Wear the ring or take it off, your decision. I want more of you." His eyes flash to my nakedness. "I want to spend time with you. In this bed, outside of this bed, in the real world, everywhere." His finger strokes along my collarbone, down my arm, and then moves across the underside of my breast. "Are you agreeable?" His thumb grazes slowly over my nipple.

"Yes. I think I'd definitely like that."

"Good. Now, remind me what else it is you like," Sebastian whispers, rolling his weight so that he is perched over me on his elbows, placing soft, seductive kisses down my neck.

"Why don't you let me show you," I reply, sliding my hand down his chest.

"Oh, baby, we are a match made in Heaven."

With the whole night stretched in front of us, I try not to think about how long this will last or if it will all end in tears and instead enjoy the sexy hot hunk of a man sharing my bed. Still, there's a tiny compartment of my mind that just won't remain quiet: Sebastian has never had a relationship with anyone. What if this isn't real and I am still part of his fake girlfriend master plan? I want to trust him, I do. But after Sam, I don't think I can take being betrayed again. Still, with his tongue doing wicked things to my body, the longevity of this situation becomes a worry for another day….

Chapter 11
Sebastian

"Shit!" I'm woken by Grace punching me in the face as she tosses and turns. How she has any energy left for fighting me in her sleep is beyond me since last night we embarked on the longest and best workout of my life. I've never slept with a woman all night before, but I can't help wonder if such a restless sleep is because of the unusual start to our real relationship.

I untangle myself from Grace's limbs, kiss her on top of her head and lay watching her for a while. Last night she was my wild Grace. All shaking thighs, incomprehensible moans and gripping my ass so tight as she climaxed that I wouldn't be surprised if she left permanent abrasions. A part of me hopes she has. Her face, beside me on the bed this morning, is a world away from last night. Spent with exhaustion, she's free from expression, blank yet the most beautiful, breathtaking vision. Her long, dark hair is splayed across the pillow, and it's so soft I find myself reaching to touch it often. Grace doesn't seem to mind, but still, hair isn't really something I've spent any time noticing on a woman before. I've hooked-up with blondes, brunettes, a couple of redheads... I never thought I had a type, but now I realise I do. It's Grace. She ticks all my boxes.

Geraldine hisses from outside the bedroom door. Grace must have freed him from his carrier during the night, so I decide he must be hungry and I leave Grace to rest while I go feed the cat. Maybe it'll help us bond since I'm not sure Geraldine likes me. Come to think of it, I don't think he much likes anyone apart from Grace and Gramps.

"Here, kitty…," I whisper-call to him, shaking a box of food I found in the cupboard. While Geraldine eats, I put on a fresh cup of coffee and hunt the kitchen for eggs and bacon. I'm ravenous after last night, and I'm guessing Grace will be too.

While the bacon fries, Geraldine approaches me and I bend and tentatively hold out my hand. He sniffs me, then pushes his face towards my hand so I can scratch beneath his chin. *You like that, huh?* I scratch more, pleased to be finally cementing a relationship with the beast that my woman adores. "Good, kitty kitty." *Good kitty kitty? What has become of me?* Geraldine flips onto his back and lets out a purr so loud the floor vibrates.

"You made friends?" I can hear the smile in Grace's voice even before I look up.

"I think we did." I return her smile, and not just because she looks fucking sensational in just my shirt, but because making her happy feels fantastic.

I bring my hand back down to Geraldine's tummy but apparently he's had enough, he hisses at me, then claws me.

Grace giggles. "Don't take it personally. He's a bit of an asshole in the morning." Then she walks up to me and kisses my shoulder. "Good morning. I think I could get used to waking up to a shirtless Sebastian making me breakfast."

I grab her ass and bring the knuckles of my other hand up to clench them between my teeth. "That ass is fucking amazing." I squeeze it again. "Let's sack off breakfast, I want a bite of your ass instead."

Grace giggles and swats my hand away, then she sits at the counter. "I'm famished. You used up all my energy last night. I need to replenish the reserves. What are you making?"

I place a coffee in front of her, and then plate up the bacon, eggs and toast.

"Dadaaa!"

"Ooh. This looks so good." Grace eats with gusto, and I sit beside her and do the same. I glance at the clock. It's almost eight and I still need to go home, shower and get changed before I start work but I feel reluctant to leave.

"How would you feel about me moving your sewing machine into my office?"

Grace laughs and I frown.

"You're serious?"

I nod.

"It's unlikely I'd get any work done with you sitting opposite me all day." She winks.

"I think that would be a fantastic advantage to the shared office space."

"It would be unfair to the other employees who don't get to spend the day looking at your gorgeous face."

"Gorgeous?" I smile, letting the compliment spread through my veins. "You're right. Maybe I should move my computer next to your desk."

"I think you should probably work from your office. But perhaps we could have lunch in the breakout room together? I could bring you a sandwich."

"I'd rather eat you in my office with the blinds down."

"Let's allow my colleagues to get used to seeing us together before we traumatise them with the knowledge we're doing it." I wink.

I tap my head with my index finger. "Fair enough, but just so you know, it's noted that you're open to the idea."

"And just so you know, Stone Enterprises take sexual harassment at work very seriously." Her tongue dips out to moisten her lips.

"You're right. We must be careful we don't get caught."

Grace shakes her head and then giggles. She stands from

her space at the counter, then grips it for support. Her face pales and her eyes fill with water.

"Grace. Are you—"

She sprints from the room into the bathroom. I follow but not in time to get to her before she locks the bathroom door. The sound of liquid hitting porcelain followed by the unmistakeable sound of dry heaves echoes through the door.

"It's okay. You go. I'll see you at work later. You don't need to be here for this."

"Grace, I'm not going anywhere, and you're not going to work today. You're clearly sick. You should see a doctor. Let me in."

"It's probably just a bug. No need to infect the poor doctor with it too. Honestly, you can go." I hear the water faucet running. "I feel better already," she says though her voice is garbled as though talking while brushing her teeth. When she comes out of the room, there is a soft sheen to her skin, but her pallor has returned to normal.

"You are on strict bed rest today," I order. Then I take out my phone and text Rosie, who is due back at work today.

"I feel tired, which is unlike me as I never get sick. My whole class at school once came down with swine flu, everyone except me. My mum made me stay home for a fortnight, we had to be careful not to pass infection onto Florence, but I was fine."

"You're a tough cookie. But everyone needs looking after sometimes." My phone pings a message that I read and then hold it out for Grace to see. "Rosie will drop off my files and laptop. I'm working from home today, your home. That way I'll be here if you need anything."

"There's really no need. I'm—" Grace sprints back to the bathroom, only this time she doesn't have time to shut the door. I rub her back while she is sick and then hand her a towel. "You should go before you catch it too," she says.

"Babe, we spent the whole night swapping spit and

sharing air. If I'm going to get it, I'm safer here rather than spreading the germs. I'm putting us both in quarantine for the next twenty-four hours."

Grace rinses her face and brushes her teeth again. I grab her hand and pull her to sit on the sofa, pulling a throw blanket over her, then I kiss the top of her head. I've never dealt with a sick woman before, but I want to take care of Grace. Part of me also wonders if I should insist on a doctor, but after checking her temperature I decide to wait and see how she is after a few hours. I sit beside her on the sofa and pull her feet up onto my lap. Grace picks up the TV controller and switches on Netflix while I rub her feet.

"Okay," she sighs. "I'm onboard with the quarantine so long as you don't stop doing that." She presses play on a romantic comedy she's found and I make myself comfortable.

"You got it, baby."

Chapter 12
Grace

When Sebastian's PA arrives to bring him some clothes and his work equipment, curiosity gets the better of me and I peek out of the window to check her out, even though Sebastian hasn't let me move from the sofa yet, despite feeling fine.

Rosie is tall and blonde with long limbs and lithe muscles. She's wearing scarlet red peep-toe shoes that elongate her legs and match her plump lips. They spend a few minutes talking in the entrance way and then Rosie hops back in her Porsche Boxster and speeds away.

Sebastian employing a super-hot PA should not piss me off. It shouldn't. It's ridiculous that it does. So, he has a hot assistant. I'm sure plenty of men do and they maintain platonic relationships with them. Still, why does she have to be so supermodel gorgeous?

"Has Rosie worked for you long?" I ask when he returns to the room.

He doesn't look up as he sets up his laptop and plugs it into the power supply. "About six months now."

"Is she a good PA?" I casually flick the page of my Sudoku book.

"Excellent actually."

"Excellent actually," I repeat and stare at the puzzle in front of me. "And is Rosie… is she single?"

I make the mistake of looking up and meeting Sebastian's gaze. His lips quip up in a smile. "I believe she is. Not that we discuss such matters. Are you… jealous?"

"Absolutely not." I shake my head. "It's no business of mine if your PA is single or is knocking boots with every guy in Heaven. She looks like she just walked out of a shampoo commercial, that's all. I hear guys like that." I return my gaze to my book but can still feel the heat from his stare.

"Knocking boots?" There's a smirk in Sebastian's voice as he moves to sit beside me on the sofa, pulling my legs up onto his lap. "You are adorable when you're jealous. There has never been anything between Rosie and me. She's great at her job, and that is where our relationship starts and stops. Besides, I'm more partial to your particular brand of shampoo."

"Oh, I wasn't worried," I lie. "It's just, what with Stone Enterprise's sexual harassment policy and all, I wouldn't want you to get into trouble."

Sebastian outright chuckles. "Thank you for your concern, but there is only one employee I am sexually attracted to."

"Oh?" I reply, casually peeking at him from the corner of my eye.

"Yes. You. But I still hope that I can convert you to a business partner. I've had Rosie bring me some research and projections. Let me invest in your idea. I can be a silent partner. You can use all my contacts. I can help you." He combs a strand of my hair between his finger and thumb. "What do you say?"

I'd never given much thought to running my own business. I don't have the start-up costs for one, and two, I have an overarching fear of failure. I've always been the same. It's why I didn't play sports at school or attend university.

"You do know your idea is good enough, don't you? With your insight and mad skills, this could be excellent?"

When he says it like that, he has me wondering if I can make a pipe dream a reality. "And you'll help me? Every step of the way? I mean, I have no idea where to even start." I bite on my lip nervously. Sebastian is a business man with a proven track record. I am a seamstress with zero experience, except a passion for craft and a zest for Sudoku.

"I honestly believe you'll be better at business than you give yourself credit, and it'd be my pleasure to work with you on this."

**

After spending the afternoon putting together a business plan with Sebastian's help, he then cooks a simple pasta dish for dinner. We dine by candlelight. Sebastian seems to prefer it that way, and it makes the simple act of eating with him feel special. The way he looks at me, like the rest of the room is just white noise and I am a symphony, sends my heart rate into overdrive. With Sam, dinner would be eaten from plates perched on our laps in front of the TV. And our conversation wouldn't amount to very much more than him asking me if he could eat the rest of my fries, or him yelling at whatever game was playing on the sports channel. With Sebastian, he asks thoughtful questions. Like my opinion of the new spring/summer range for Stone's designer interior range. He listens intently as I reel off the pieces I like and picks up on the pieces I don't care for. He doesn't impose his opinion on me or tell me I'm wrong when my conclusion doesn't match his. He just nods thoughtfully and changes the debate. His eyes gleam pridefully as I reel off my notes on the competition's styling and with his undivided attention and encouragement, I explain my view as to what Stone's excelling in and where I think improvements can be made. And even though we talk in depth about business, it doesn't feel like we are avoiding the elephant in the room… our relationship status. It's two minds discussing similar interests.

I insist on helping Sebastian clear away the dishes. He's shown no sign of being sick and I feel fine. But once again, as soon as I am done eating, nausea engulfs me. This time I manage to lock the bathroom door in time so I can puke in private.

"Grace, let me in. I've already seen you vomit. There's no need to hide this from me. I could hold your hair back?"

As much as I love it when he strokes my hair, even pulling it up to smell it sometimes, he need not witness this. "I'm fine, really. Go see if you can finish the Sudoku on page 38. It's a hard one."

Once I have rinsed my face and mouth, I open the mirrored cabinet above the vanity looking for some pain relief for the pounding in my head that is on the brink of a horrendous headache. What I see is the small, blue box of tampons staring back at me as if mocking me.

I'm good with numbers. I can complete an evil rated Sudoku puzzle in under thirty minutes. I was times table champion three years running in middle school. But I cannot for the life of me work out how many days it has been since my last period.

Sebastian taps on the door three times, and his silky-smooth voice requests entry once again.

"Just a minute," I holler, closing the cabinet door and scanning the room for any sign of evidence that I may be pregnant as if suddenly it's so obvious it's written on the walls.

Pregnant.

I can't be.

I haven't slept with Sam for over six months. I look down at my stomach. Definitely not six months gone. More like a big bowl of pasta and a KitKat too many. So that only leaves….

"C'mon, let me in. I'm getting worried out here."

Shit.

Five weeks ago I had very hot sex with a very hot Sebastian Stone. I was moderately inebriated, I suspect he was too, but we definitely used a condom.

"I'm banging down the door if you don't answer me, Grace."

"Okay, okay, I'm coming."

"Thank God. You okay?" Sebastian asks. The growing concern that the sexy bastard in front of me knocked me up, coupled with or without morning sickness is making me feel even more nauseated. The room has been vacuumed of oxygen and I feel dizzy.

"I'm fine. You need to go. I need to be alone. Just a headache. I'll call you tomorrow. I'll probably be fine by tomorrow." My words are choppy and sharp, and I have no idea if I am repeating the same words over and over because of my inability to think straight. I pull Sebastian by his arm to the front door without making eye contact.

I open the door as wide as it will go. The cool, outside air is not as delicious as the spicy cologne Sebastian wears—the one I have gotten used to and could tell apart from a million others—but since that scent is clouding my already confused mind, I suck in the cool fresh air and it's a welcome relief.

"You mind if I put my shoes on before you throw me out?"

"I'm not throwing you out. I need to get some rest. You've been here all day." I pick up Sebastian's shoes from the floor and his car keys from the console table and thrust them at him.

"I'm sorry I've imposed," he replies coldly. I don't meet his gaze but he fixes this by lifting my chin to look in my eyes. I'm bare beneath his scrutiny and powerless to stop myself looking up into his big brown eyes. My swallow is an audible gulp. He looks confused, worried even. "What's wrong? You're shaking and you look terrified."

Which is exactly how he will feel when he finds out.

I drag my eyes away from the hurt expression on his face and focus on Geraldine who is throwing me a sideways glare from the doorway to the kitchen. "I'm going to rest. Nothing to worry about. I'll call you." Sebastian lets me push him out of the door and I close it behind him. Then I run to the bathroom to be sick.

**

I didn't rest. I tossed and turned all night. I came to Heaven for a fresh start to put Sam's bullshit behind me and stand on my own two feet.

Sebastian has been clear. He doesn't want a relationship. *Seeing where this goes*, is not synonymous with a proper, committed relationship. He's never spent an extended period of time romantically with a woman before. There is no way this relationship can have a future. He doesn't want kids. He said as much.

I am an idiot for possibly getting knocked up by my boss's, boss's, boss.

My day begins with hugging the lavatory and then calling in work to tell them I am sick. I text Willow to reassure her I am okay and then type out no less than seven messages to Sebastian. I can't bring myself to press Send on any of them. I treated him badly last night, and he is bound to be wondering what on earth is going on. However, I know he has a busy day at work today and also a meeting in the city, so I have ample time to put my plan into place.

I pull up at Heaven's only pharmacy fifteen minutes before it closes. I've never needed to come here before, but I pass it every day on my way to work. I wanted to come earlier but the sickness took its toll, and I decided I couldn't risk leaving the house until I had kept down a full piece of toast for at least one hour.

The car park is quiet and I wonder if waiting until later in the day was one of my brighter ideas. Everyone is probably travelling home from work by now and the store looks as empty as the car park. The mechanical doors open with a whoosh, and like a secret agent I enter and scan the store for customers.

I don't know many people in this town but still, I've been privy to enough gossip since I arrived to know that small towns talk. And as a new person, I'm almost guaranteed to be hot news. Especially since word will have gotten around that I am dating the town's beloved Sebastian Stone.

The engagement ring on my finger glows like a beacon. *Fiancé.* Not just dating. As far as the town knows, I am his soon-to-be wife.

I start on the first aisle, moving past the hair colours, perming lotion and shampoos. The second aisle is full of men's styling products and a luxurious display of gloves, which I hide behind as I recheck for locals who may know me, and then, when I get to the third aisle I find the pregnancy tests right beside the condoms, which is ironic because had the condom worked I would not be in this predicament. I scoop up three different brands of tests and casually wonder if the condom manufacturers also have shares in pregnancy tests. They say you can't trust big pharma companies, and I'm wondering if there's some truth in that statement.

There's no queue to pay and just one older lady serving. She's filing her nails and looking decidedly bored as she waits for the clock to chime for home time. I pick up a multipack of mints, not that they will hide what I am about to put on the conveyor belt, but I hope that it will distract from the pregnancy tests so that I won't become the gossip in this small town where everyone knows everyone's business.

Dammit. I should've driven out of town.

"That'll be twenty-six-forty," the cashier says without looking up.

I have my credit card poised for action, waving it beneath her nose, hoping she'll hurry.

"Sorry, cash only." She points to a sign at the front of the shop and my jaw drops.

"That's okay, I can get that. Grace, honey, is that you?"

Perspiration trickles into my hair line as the shop assistant loads my items into what must surely be the smallest, most transparent plastic bag in the world. I turn around slowly.

"Betty, thank you. I can send you the cash via PayPal?"

Betty looks at me strangely. "It's okay, honey, don't worry about it. You're family now." She smiles warmly then her eyes pause on the bag.

"They're for my cat!" I startle both the cashier and Betty with my Tourette-like bark.

Betty's hand lands on my forearm and she gives it a squeeze that makes me want to lean in for a hug. "Well, I'm sure Geraldine's breath will be minty fresh once he's gotten through all those—" She squints at the bag. "—triple Mints and Clear Blues."

I snatch up the bag and snake it behind my back, then step away so the cashier can give Betty her change. I promise to pay her back, to come see her soon, and silently say a prayer that she actually thinks I'm putting Geraldine on a strict diet of mints. It's better than her knowing I got knocked up by her practically adopted grandson. Then I floor it home to discover my destiny.

Chapter 13
Sebastian

"Will it be a big wedding, with all the neighbours invited?" Mrs McClusky asks, her voice laden with hope. I've been standing outside Grace's place for fifteen minutes and getting interrogated by Mrs McClusky for fourteen of those.

"Yes. Sure, why not? You'll receive an invite when we name the day."

What am I saying *when we name the day*? Grace will kill me for saying that. Especially after she threw me out last night and today her car is gone. Has she skipped town? Did I put too much pressure on her? I've gone balls to the wall with her before she was ready. She warned me at the start, she didn't want to get involved or break my heart, course at the time the idea seemed laughable. Now, well, my heart is fucking hurting already, and she hasn't even called things off. *Yet.*

Shit, what if she's done with me?

McClusky has been whittling on and I haven't been listening, but despite that she seems to think I've agreed to something. "Thank you. You two will make the loveliest bride and groom in Heaven. So remember, don't sit me next to Donald Gibbons, he never shuts up and I can't get a single word in edgeways. William Drake, he's who I want to sit next to as he always gives me a ride home when I ask. But not Donald, no Donald wouldn't think to offer a lady a ride even if his pacemaker depended on it."

I hear the faint sound of a car turning down the street and I lean my head around McClusky. It's Grace, thank God. I wait for her to switch off the engine, then ignore McClusky to go open her door. I startle Grace, like she didn't see me approach. She snatches a plastic bag off her passenger seat and slides out the car. She smiles at me, though it's not her usual easy smile. It's strained, like she's nervous.

Shit. She's going to dump me.

"You okay?" Nerves strangle my voice.

"Yes. Feeling much better. Hi, Mrs McClusky, you got your shopping list all done for me?" She smiles warmly at the old lady who straddles the path between Grace's car and her front door.

"I'll have it done by tomorrow like usual. Make sure the bananas are green. Last week they were brown by Wednesday."

Grace smiles back and tells the ungrateful old cow she will do that. I follow Grace to her front door and am relieved she lets me in. Grace slips off her dainty ballerina style pumps and slides them into the shoe rack. I follow suit.

"I left my laptop and files here last night. Not that I needed them today, but I thought I better stop them cluttering up your space."

She smiles nervously, swinging her arms behind her back. "I'm just going into the bathroom. I won't be a tick."

My hand reaches out to her forehead. Her temperature feels normal. "Any more sickness?" I check.

"Just a little." She spins on her heel and enters the bathroom, closing the door behind her. There's a knock at the door, so I loop back to answer it.

"Well, shit, you took your time. I just had a verbal assault from McClusky for parking one millimetre over her driveway. Crazy old bat doesn't even own a car."

I recognise the woman as Willow, as she brushes past me and she walks in. I know Willow in many capacities though we've never been friendly. She's a long-time resident of Heaven and was a few years below me at school. She briefly dated my friend Ethan, and she's also the woman who Grace was in the bar with the night we met. Most recently I interviewed her for the manager's position at the Stone factory, though I am yet to inform her that her application was successful.

"Grace! You in? I came to check on you, and I bought you some grapes. They'll need eating today as they're starting to pucker." She walks right into the kitchen, and I follow. Grace walks out of the bathroom, and we all stand at the counter.

"You going to introduce me, then?" She waggles her eyebrows at Grace who blushes. The colour in her cheeks is a welcome change from her recent greyish pallor, and for that I immediately warm to Willow.

"You already know him. He interviewed you a few days ago and you used to date his friend."

"I wouldn't call a few drunken hook-ups with Ethan before he left town, 'dating his friend.' And this is outside of work; I can hardly call him Mr Stone here, can I?"

"Willow, this is my friend, Sebastian," she says, placating her friend.

"Friend?" Willow and I both question at the exact same moment.

Grace chews her lip. "You know what I mean."

I let the comment slide, even though the suggestion that I am a mere *friend* confirms what I hoped was way off the mark. She's going to dump me, and it'll hurt like hell.

Willow asks how Grace is feeling and then, once she's satisfied Grace is okay, begins rehashing what we missed at work today. Willow is an animated flurry of information and I get the impression that usually the girls would banter back and forth, but that today, Grace's heart's not in it.

I bend down and pick up Geraldine, who is rubbing his ass against my leg. *At least someone seems fond of me today.* I perch him in one hand holding him under his butt and stroke the spot he likes beneath his ear with my other hand. He purrs like a Harley Davidson on a drag track, and Grace's face softens as her face tilts up and she watches me stroke Geraldine with a big, beautiful smile on her face. That is until her face becomes stricken around the same time that I feel warm spurts of liquid fill my hand.

"Did Geraldine just take a piss in Sebastian's hand?" Willow guffaws.

Suspecting she might be right, I put Geraldine down into his litter tray and rush to the bathroom. Cat piss is like a bad reputation once it soaks in you can never truly get the smell gone.

I hear Grace yell, "Don't go in the bathroom!" but it's too late since I'm already in here. I slide off my jacket, throwing it on the floor, and allow the warm water to run over my hands and over the sleeve of my shirt. I apply a large handful of soap from the dispenser onto both my hand and sleeve. That's when I notice three white plastic, rectangular devices. Three innocent, unsophisticated gadgets, each one with either a line, a cross, and the third one, the one that thinks it's better than the rest, brazenly announces the word: Pregnant.

I lift the third one up, bringing it closer to my eyes so I can study it. I'm unsure if the word is spelt correctly or if maybe it means something different to what they taught me in sex education.

"Don't touch that," Grace calls from behind me.

I turn to face her, test still in my hand. Her face looks pained, worried. I try and relax the shocked look that is surely coating my face and instantly feel like an asshole. Grace must be terrified.

I soften my voice and try to confirm with my eyes that even though I am shocked, I am not angry. "I'm not afraid of a pregnancy test, Grace."

At the commotion, Willow enters the hallway and stands behind Grace, mouth agape.

Grace grimaces and her eyes lock on mine in a pleading, apologetic stare. "It's just… that's the end I peed on."

I hold it for a second longer, committing the word to memory before I throw it in the trashcan beside the vanity and rinse my still soapy hands.

"Is that… are you… holy fucking mother Mary… Excuse the pun. I'll leave you guys to it. Call me later." Willow pulls Grace into a hug, whispers something into her ear, and then she leaves.

I perch on the side of Grace's tub, and stare at the two remaining pregnancy tests.

"I guess there's no chance that all three could be wrong?" My eyes flick up to meet Grace's and her lips part, allowing me a glimpse at her pink tongue.

"They're positive?" She strides forwards and stares at the tests. Her eyes are wide and she clutches the basin for support. I stand and wrap my arms around her waist, stroking her hair so that her head rests on my chest. "Shit. I wondered, but I didn't know. I'm… There's… A baby…."

"Is it…?"

"Yes. It's yours. Sam was six months ago. There's been no one else."

I nod even though she can't see me. I knew that was the answer even before I asked.

"And do you want to—"

"Yes. It's unexpected, but I know I can do this. I don't think I could—"

"I understand. So, we're—"

"Going to be parents."

"Shit," we both say in sync.

"You don't have to—"

"I do. I want to. This baby is mine. Him or her will know their father."

Grace nods and a tear spills over her lower lash. I catch

it and wipe it away with my thumb, drawing her face to look up to mine as I do. "It will be okay—"

"I didn't do it on purpose. We used a condom. I'm sure we did." She shakes her head.

"We didn't the third time. We'd run out by then, and neither of us seemed to want to stop. This is my fault."

She looks at me blankly as though her thoughts are trying to remember back to that night, then she gasps. "Backwards cowgirl."

A smile breaks through my stoic expression. "Yes. Backwards cowgirl followed by the pretzel, if I remember correctly."

We both burst into a cackle of laughter and Grace's eyes light up with joy, giving her an angelic, beautiful glow.

I'm in a state of shock, but the primary emotion I feel is relief. Relief that my assumption that Grace was dumping me today was way off the mark.

I didn't think I wanted kids, but that decision was founded on the belief that I didn't want a relationship. I now want a relationship, but only if it's with Grace, which makes bringing a child into the world, a child who is both hers and mine seem like the most fantastic union there ever was.

I can't stop myself, my hand cups her chin and I draw her into a long and tender kiss. Grace turns in my arms and leans up on her tiptoes. My hands glide down and grab her sweet ass, lifting her up so her legs can wrap around my waist. Three long strides and we're in her bedroom, me closing a pissed-off looking Geraldine out on the other side of the door as I shut it with my toe.

Whenever Grace and I have been intimate, it's been hard and frenzied, an act of pure lust, but this time, I gently spread her out on the bed. I want to take my sweet time with her. Explore every inch of her sexy body. Sex doesn't feel enough, I want to be closer, more intimate than ever before. If I could climb inside her then I would, I want her that much.

There's a sultry, hungry look in Grace's eyes as she

watches me peel off her jeans. I lose my suit trousers and unbutton my shirt, crawling across the bed to pull off Grace's shirt. She's wearing innocent looking white underwear, but the look on her face is anything but innocent. I lean over Grace and our lips meet. A slow, leisurely make-out session ensues. I'm rock hard and my balls are fit to burst, but still I won't rush. I take my time with her body, making her call out my name and fist my hair as I taste every inch of her, ending with her hidden nub.

I allow Grace to take control and she climbs astride me, rocking back and forth in a slow dance that puts her gorgeous tits in my face and makes my balls throb for release. Our eyes are open, unyielding and mesmerised by one another's faces. She's perfect. I'm not sure how I didn't realise it before now, but now that I recognise my feelings for her they seem obvious.

"I love you." My voice is strangled with emotion, my body consumed with the need for release.

"I love you," she says with an almost surprised look on her face.

Hearing Grace say those three little words, feeling their meaning with her here, connected to me in every sense of the word is my undoing. Grace rocks faster as I thrust into her. Her hands are everywhere, gripping my hair and driving her nails into my shoulders. I take her mouth with mine, pushing my tongue in and tasting her as my balls clench, my cock pulsates, and my cum fills her. Even after the final spasms of pleasure have passed we remain fixed to one another, me pulling tendrils of her hair through my fingers and Grace stroking my back.

We have plenty to discuss, but for now, just being close to one another, knowing there is a future for us growing inside of Grace fills me with a sense of permanence that until now I didn't know existed.

"I'm going to take such good care of you, Grace Harper. You, peanut, and Geraldine, you're my family now."

Grace lifts her head off my shoulder and kisses the tip

of my nose. "One day at a time, okay. Just a few days ago you told me you didn't want a family. A part of me still wonders if you might change your mind."

"Baby, one day at a time, for the next eighty years, I'll prove to you that I stick around. I see things through, and most of all I'm doing it because I love you."

Her eyes glisten, and she swallows loudly. I brush my lips against hers and tell her again that I love her. That I'm sticking around and that she can count on me. Now I just have to figure out how I can prove it.

Chapter 14

Grace

"You promised Mrs McClusky that you would marry me wearing organza and satin *like a traditional bride*? She said you'd make sure I sat her next to William? William hates Mrs McClusky. I can't believe you would agree to all that!" I huff, walking back through the door having delivered Mrs McClusky's groceries—Sebastian offered to do it, but since it was only a small bag, he let me, and it relieved him to avoid Mrs McClusky. I join him as he unpacks our groceries after our trip to the supermarket.

"I don't know what I agreed to. That woman never stops talking. She ground me down. Don't tell me you haven't felt the effects of her whittling on; that's how you've ended up doing that woman's grocery shopping despite her being perfectly capable of doing it herself." Sebastian raises a thick brow at me, daring me to call him out.

"That's not the point," I argue and push my bottom lip out as I consider a counterargument, but Sebastian butts in before I have the chance.

"It bodes well for me that you are more annoyed about the seating plan than you are about getting married." He puts down the can of beans in his hands and takes my left hand. "Let's make this real."

I glance at the dazzling diamond that proudly sits on a platinum band. The most beautiful ring I ever saw, that despite its false pretences, I can't bring myself to remove, and I brush aside his comment. "Let's focus on one thing at a time. You have a habit of rushing ahead with whatever shiny thing has gotten your attention. We need to work on your communication skills." I throw Sebastian an "I mean business stare" which he counters with puppy dog eyes and a cute smile.

"Women like men that take charge, don't they?"

"Women like men who listen and compromise. You're too used to getting your own way all the time. If we are working on being a couple, you need to learn to consult me. Equals, remember?"

"You are my equal. I even let you take control. Last night I was all over being dominated." He flashes me a sexy, cocky grin and a wink that sends a flood of heat straight to my lady parts.

I hold up my hands and count all the ways his communication has been lacking. "The fake engagement. Calling my parents and arranging to meet them. Golf with my dad, which is in two days. Sam's interview. Dinner with your grandpa. Telling Mrs McClusky what fabric my dress would be and telling her she can choose who she sits beside at the wedding. I'm running out of fingers!"

Sebastian takes a seat at the counter and his eyes rest on mine. "You don't like that stuff?" His eyes turn down and looks sad, his manly good looks turning boyish.

"I do appreciate the gesture behind some of that stuff, but if we are going to figure this situation out, you need to start thinking of us as a team. Consult before we act. You're used to flying solo, and this is new to both of us. Do you think you can try to turn over a new leaf?"

Sebastian chews on his lower lip as he considers. Then his arms snake around me and he pulls me towards him, gently stroking the smooth skin of my abdomen beneath my jumper. His eyes are intense with emotion, more serious than I've ever seen them. "From now on, I'll talk to you first before I do anything daft. You and peanut are my most precious things now. I'm trying really hard not to fuck this up, but it terrifies me that it's inevitable. Like something this good can't possibly last."

I pull my arms up around his neck and hold him close to me. He smells like soap and wood. His body feels hard, but warm and safe. He pulls me into his arms. "I love you." Sebastian kisses the top of my head and whispers those same three words back to me. "Nothing good comes without work, but we can't live in fear. No matter what the future holds, we put peanut first, always."

Sebastian chuckles a laugh and pulls away just enough so he can look in my eyes. "You used my nickname."

"Yeah, I like it. It's cute, like his daddy."

Sebastian's eyes light up. "You think it's a boy?"

"I don't know, but I can't keep thinking of him as it."

"We'll find out Wednesday. I scheduled a doctor visit for you. After, we can have lunch, and then there's this great house up on Sandford Street by the beach. It has this amazing view and—"

"Stop! What were we just talking about," I say, exasperated.

"Shit. I was listening. I will compromise." He closes his eyes, then looks at me, cocking his head and holding his palms up. "I made those appointments before our chat. Next time, I'll call you first, and we'll discuss it. And if you don't like the house, then we'll look for a different one."

"Sebastian. We have fake dated for a week and have been seeing where it goes for three days. Slow down. We are not moving in together or getting married yet."

Sebastian nods and looks disappointed, then his lips lift in a smile. "Yet?" He pulls me into a kiss and squeezes my ass. "For now, I can live with yet."

**

The next day, we meet my parents and Florence for lunch. Despite me trying to downplay the engagement, my parents, sister, and Sebastian are a flurry of wedding chatter, and I get caught up in their excitement.

"Oh, Grace. Look at that chapel. That's the place. It's perfect." My mum smiles and wipes her eyes, handing back Sebastian's phone with the Heaven Chapel website.

I was twelve when I planned my first wedding. They had cancelled outside play at school because of the rain, so I attended maths club in the school cafeteria. That's how I came to sit beside Martin Brown that day, and two days later he asked me out on a date. I was sure he was the boy I would marry, and so I designed my dress, picked my flowers, and chose my bridesmaids. He was my first kiss and the first boy that I ever told I loved. We dated for three weeks before, that summer, my sister got sick, and I ended up spending all my time at the hospital with her. Martin waited for me the whole summer. He'd post love letters through my bedroom window for me to find when I got home from the hospital each night. We'd planned to go to McDonalds at the end of the week. My mum, who was sure my sister was improving, assured me missing one visit would be fine, but on the day of my date, Mum suddenly broke down in tears as she and Dad explained the doctors made a mistake. They got it wrong. My sister's condition had worsened and we immediately needed to prepare to say our goodbyes. Suddenly I didn't care about my date with Martin, but my mum made me call him to tell him I couldn't go to McDonalds. But I didn't tell him I couldn't go. I told him we were over. I just couldn't bear to feel any amount of joy or happiness. It felt wrong, worse than wrong it felt criminal. The pain of losing Martin was miniscule compared to the pain I felt encapsulated in losing my sister. Years later, following many close calls, Florence finally beat that tragic disease, and I never planned another wedding, and I never went back to maths club.

"Grace, are you even listening? I said we'll all go shopping to that new designer village in Hatton," my sister announces. "You have a big credit card, don't you?" Florence cheekily asks Sebastian.

"I'll pay for my little girl's wedding. It's tradition." My dad nods firmly.

"Wait, dad, you don't have to—"

"I'll pay. It's the least I can do. Grace has changed how I feel about, well, everything." Sebastian looks surprised, shaking his head as though he still can't believe how many things have changed. His hand unconsciously reaches for my stomach, but with my parents and sister sitting opposite us, I have no choice but to swat it away.

I'm not ready to tell people until the doctor has verified everything is okay and peanut is safe in there. I can't protect my parents and sister from life, but when I tell them, I want to be sure that they have nothing extra to worry about.

Sebastian bites his lip and shakes his head as though he realises his faux pas. I throw him a smile, showing that it's okay.

When we leave the restaurant, and Sebastian drives past Heaven, I ask him where he is taking me.

"Well, you already agreed to this, so you can't be mad."

My eyes narrow curiously. "What have you done?"

Chapter 15
Sebastian

"A weekend away? What about Geraldine?"

"Taken care of. I've packed a bag for you. Mrs McClusky has Geraldine for the next two nights, and I've promised to pay for the deep clean if he poops, pees or spews on any part of her home. Though being honest, I think McClusky was angling for me to pay for the decorators to come in if Gerry so much as hisses at one of her porcelain dolls."

She sits back in the car and chews over my speech.

"What about golf with my dad and your gramps tomorrow? Are you bailing on them?"

"Nope. I booked you in at the hotel spa for a relaxing massage. Willow and Florence are meeting you there at ten."

Grace nods and I adore watching the smile creep in and take over her face.

"What if massage isn't good for preg—"

"Already googled it and phoned ahead to the spa. They do a special pregnancy treatment which I've booked for you, and they promise to be discreet." I keep my eyes on the road but can't help glancing at her to check her reaction.

"You sure? Spa treatments can be expensive."

I pull into the hotel and switch off the engine. "Baby,

there is nothing I want to spend money on more than taking care of you. From now on, you want anything, anything at all, then it's yours. I thought we should start with your car. It'll be hell trying to get a car seat and stroller in that thing. And what if you break down? And peanut is due a feed, or it's cold out? It could be hours before recovery gets to you. Also, I've been googling, and babies need loads of stuff. I'm not sure your car will cope."

Grace's hand stretches out to squeeze mine.

"Slow. Down."

"I am going slow. Not as slow as your car, but still, this is me going slow."

Grace laughs and then glances at the stately hotel in front of us.

Her eyes light up and her full pink lips pop open. "Wow. This place is fancy." I let her blatant subject change go for now.

My hand slides to her thigh. "It is. You want to see the view from the four-poster bed?"

Grace turns and looks up at me seductively through her thick lashes. "Oh, I want to see the bed, all right. But I've got quite a different view in mind."

My swallow echoes through the car. "I was hoping you'd say that."

**

We spend the afternoon making love. I'm sure there's a soft swell to Grace's stomach, but she laughs and says it's too early to show and that it's probably just gas—which, no way my girl farts. She always smells fucking amazing. And her breasts. From the start I was convinced they were the finest tits in town, but now I've reconsidered that to include the whole damned world.

I get out of the shower and am about to sling a towel around my waist when I pause in front of the mirror. The door is open and I can see Grace sitting in front of the dresser, curling her hair before we go to dinner in the restaurant downstairs. She looks stunning in the long emerald dress I picked out for her, and my dick instantly hardens. Lately, it just won't stay down. I'm permanently hard whenever she is within fifty feet.

"Are you thinking about your dick, again?" Grace stands and gives me an approving head to toe stare.

"No. Yes. A little. Do you think if he's a boy, he'll inherit my genes?" I grin at her and tug my head towards my junk.

"One can only hope." She snorts. "But hopefully not your obsession with it."

"Hey, there's not a guy out there who doesn't think about these things."

Grace laughs. "Perfectly healthy, I'm sure." She looks down, and her eyes rest on my package. The tip of her tongue darts out to innocently moisten her lips, and my cock clenches with desire. "Do you think we have time before the reservation…."

Before she's finished her sentence, I am unzipping her dress and lowering her back onto the bed. I briefly wonder how I'll ever get anything done in a day when all I want to do is be inside Grace every moment of every day, but then her hands wrap around my cock and all thoughts about anything except how fucking good she looks, how divine she smells, and how fucking delicious she tastes consume my every thought.

Fuck, I love this woman.

**

Gramps and Grace's dad, Phil, meet me at the golf course on Sunday while Grace enjoys her spa day with Willow and her sister.

My game is on point and I'm on fire, as I stomp home the best score by a mile. Everything is perfect right now. Nothing feels unconquerable.

"You look like the cat that got the cream," Phil says as

we prop up the bar on the nineteenth hole.

"He looks like a man in love," my gramps replies.

Instinct urges me to deny it, but I can't. "I... This is new territory to me." I shrug.

"Young Sebastian was a reluctant husband, until he found your daughter," Gramps replies to Phil.

"Have to say, I was surprised Grace got engaged so soon after meeting you, Sebastian." Phil takes a sip of his beer and I wait eagerly for him to qualify his comment. "Grace has always been a flight risk. After she moved to Heaven, a part of me hoped it'd be short-lived. That she'd return home to us, but I guess now she'll be remaining in Heaven."

Static runs down my spine. "A flight risk?" I ask casually.

Phil snuffs a laugh out of his nostrils. "Grace has only had a couple of boyfriends over the years, but whenever it's gone wrong or she's got spooked, she's always fled. I had hoped when she ran off from that loser, Sam, that the wind would bring her home, but then she fell in love with Heaven, Stone Enterprises and Sebastian here." Phil lifts his beer and clinks it against mine. "Still, you seem like a great guy; you just make sure you take care of my little girl."

"Always," I reply. Gramps watches our exchange with interest and then suggests another round of drinks. The conversation continues, but at the back of my mind I am dissecting Phil's comment.

Is Grace a flight risk?

I've been coming on strong and she hasn't run, *yet*. Maybe I should back off and give her time to adjust to our situation. If I don't, I could fuck this up by pushing her away.

Act cool, Sebastian, and you may just end up with everything you never knew you wanted.

Chapter 16
Grace

Florence stretches out on the lounger by the pool and takes a sip of her champagne. "This place is amazing. Have I died and woken up in Heaven?"

"Not funny, Flo!" I deadpan and Willow gives us both a strange look.

"My sister doesn't like it when I make dead jokes. Because I almost died a few times." Florence laughs.

Willow arches her brows. "I guess if anything takes the fun out of a dead joke, it's almost dying." She shakes her head and turns her attention back to the menu. "I think I will have the hot stone massage followed by the million-dollar facial. It's been a tough week, but now I got my dream job, I'm feeling fancy."

I gasp. "He gave you the job? Whoop. That's awesome. You were the best person for the job by a straight mile." I lean up and give Willow a squeeze. "I bet it pisses Dominic off!"

I let go of Willow and she lies back on the daybed, wagging her finger as she says, "He'll get over it. That guy is about to learn there's a new boss in town and she doesn't take no shit!"

"To taking no shit," my sister says and we all clink glasses. "Hey, why ain't you drinking?"

I make up the best excuse I can think of and hope Flo buys it. Willow already knows I'm pregnant, but I texted her earlier and asked her not to mention it. Until I know everything is okay, I can't bring myself to worry my family. "Oh, me? On a diet. You know, for the wedding."

"You don't need to go on a diet, and you didn't even set a date yet." Flo looks suspicious so I do my best to change the subject. "Think of it as cutting back. Sebastian is ultra-fit. He joined us both up at the gym. And I'm trying to make better choices. You know how I love a fad gimmick. This time it's diet and exercise."

Flo nods, and then Willow helps me out. "You know what my neighbour lost thirty pounds doing? The sex diet. Which is not a diet at all. More really is less with this one. You screw three times a day. Breakfast, lunch and dinner, and by the end of the work outs, not only have you burnt a ton of calories, but you're too fucked to bother cooking a meal!"

We all cackle laughing and then my sister says, "Where do I sign up? I'm in the midst of man drought and I'm getting thirsty!"

"I feel your pain," Willow agrees then her eyes flick to mine. "Oh, you sit there all smug, Grace. You're probably getting it seven times a day with Seb, huh? I'm glad you guys are now dating for real."

My sister's eyes pop from Willow's to mine. "For real?"

Willow's face drops into an oh-shit-I-said-too-much look. I grin at her to let her know it's okay. "We started out as more of a business arrangement. But it's totally okay, because now we are on track proper."

Flo puts down her champagne and sits up so she can analyse my expression, my posture, and my body language. Hell, I wouldn't put it past her to wheel out a lie detector. "A business agreement? Okay, so you better start from the beginning and leave nothing out."

I let out a nervous chortle. "It's fine, we just—"

"Grace, spill," she demands. And so I tell her everything. The news of the baby is the only part I don't share. It's therapeutic, explaining everything from the start. It also helps me find perspective and realise where Sebastian and I are at—objectively. It's not something I can do when I'm with him, because being with Sebastian is like taking drugs. The high is so high I never want to come down, but still, in the back of my mind, I'm terrified that what goes up must come down.

"So let me get this straight. You agreed to date him so he could get his hands on his grandfather's company, he made you engaged without your permission, and now you love him?"

I nod. "That about sums it up."

"Grace, that is fucked up. Did he get the business yet?"

I shake my head. Flo opens then closes her mouth as though she was going to say something but thought before she yelled.

"Say what's on your mind, Flo."

"How do you know it's real now? You told him you wanted out and then suddenly he feels actual feelings. How much is this business worth?"

I shrug, but Willow answers for me. "Eighteen point six billion."

"What?" Flo and I both shriek as our heads ping in Willow's direction, cartoon style.

"It's true. Biggest textile operation worldwide."

"Fuck," Flo and I say in unison.

"Babe, I'm sure he loves you, really I am. You are an amazing, beautiful woman and he'd be a moron not to love you, and I don't know him, but neither do you. Didn't he date that supermodel, Echo Matiz? Are you sure he's ready to settle down from the billionaire playboy lifestyle?" Flo doesn't look convinced at all. Her face falls like she feels bad for me. She takes a steadying breath, softens her tone, and adds, "All I'm saying is, that is a lot of money, and people have done much worse things than fake a romance to get their hands on that kind of cash. Just be careful. I don't want to see you get hurt again."

"I do know him, and it's really not like that," I say. "And besides, since Arthur hasn't even given him the company even after we got engaged, I think Sebastian would still be with me, even if the company was off the table. He hasn't posted anything on social media since we decided to give this relationship a try. Maybe, I've become more important than getting his hands on Stone Enterprises."

"Maybe." Flo smiles, a flat smile that doesn't reach her eyes. "I hope so," she says and firms up her smile. "You know how cynical I am when it comes to matters of the heart. I'm sure he is just as invested in you as he is in the company."

A stunning spa employee in a black uniform with gold embellished branding appears by our side. Her posture is straight, her lips perfectly painted. "Mrs Stone, it's time for your massage."

"Mrs Stone?" I repeat.

"That's what it says on the booking." She smiles politely.

I chortle a nervous laugh. "He's always doing dumb stuff like this." I shake my head.

"Just so long as that's all the dumb stuff he's up to," my sister replies as I follow the masseuse through the spa to the treatment room.

Even though massages should be relaxing, I can't make my muscles untighten. What if I'm missing the signs again, like I did with Sam? I think Sebastian loves me. It feels real. Is that because I want it to be real, or perhaps my hormones are at work?

I decide my sister is right, I need to be cautious. I want things to work out. But it's not just me anymore, and peanut deserves a stable home with trustworthy parents.

**

"You ready?" I ask, standing outside East Angleford's fanciest, private maternity clinic. Sebastian met me here because he has been working in the city the past couple of days "tying up loose ends."

"As I'll ever be," he replies, takes my hand, and then we walk through the electric doors. My palms are sweaty and I'm nervous as hell, but Sebastian's firm grip wrapped around my hand, bolsters my courage.

The hospital is well signposted, and it doesn't take long until we are seated outside Doctor Craner's office, waiting to be seen.

"So have you been okay these past few days? Any more sickness?"

"I told you on the phone, much better. Tuesday I even managed to eat a tuna salad. Although, I am peeing all the time. The cleaner even put up a notice at work, asking people to stop stealing the toilet paper." I laugh and glance at Sebastian, but he's looking at his phone. He seems distant today.

"Mr and Mrs Stone?" The receptionist calls and angles her head to the office door. "You can go through now."

"Mrs Stone?" I whisper-yell at him.

Sebastian shrugs and throws me an innocent smile, which I shake my head to. He puts his arm around me and then whispers into my ear, "I like how it sounds, Mrs Stone." I narrow my eyes. The mixed signals I am receiving today are giving me whiplash, but in truth, I've missed him, and hearing him call me Mrs Stone sends a zing of pleasure through me and I pass him a nervous, tight-lipped smile. "I'll stop using that name. I know you're not ready." He nods at me resolute.

The doctor is an older lady, round and jolly with an infectious smile. She refers to us both as Mum and Dad, like we don't have other names. I don't complain because Mum and Dad sounds nice, like it somehow makes peanut official.

Once I've removed my bottom layer of clothes and

pulled the sheet over me in the chair, Doctor Craner and Sebastian come through to the examination room and the doctor gestures for me to put my legs in the stirrups.

"So, Mum thinks she's about seven weeks?"

I nod.

"Okay, well let's find out."

Sebastian grips my hand, hard, like he's the one having what looks like a stick with a condom on it shoved up his hoo-ha. I try to relax, but it's no easy task.

"Can we find out the sex today?" Sebastian looks down at me. "Can you imagine Gramps face if it was a boy? Another Stone heir." His smile is strained, and a bead of sweat slides down the edge of his hairline. There are dark circles under his eyes, and I wonder if he's been as worried about today as I have?

"It's far too early to tell the sex. But you might want to discuss whether to find out at a later scan. Some parents prefer to wait."

The room falls quiet as we wait for an image or sound, anything to indicate peanut is in there and thriving. The only sound is the beat of my heart, rushing through my ears, pulsating through my entire body as I wait. Perspiration creeps down the back of my neck and even though the room is warm, I'm hyper aware of the cool air against my inner thighs.

"Takes a little while sometimes to—and there she is." The doctor turns the screen towards us and turns up the sound. The room is filled with a swooshing sound with obvious beats picking out a strong and fast heartbeat. "Sounds perfect," Doctor Craner reassures. "You see here, on the screen." She points to a perfect peanut shape.

I can't speak because my throat is constricted by a tennis ball lump and a content sob is threatening to escape.

"That's your baby, and she looks exactly as she should at this stage. A viable pregnancy and hopefully a textbook one." I feel Doctor Craner move the device within me, and then she peers closer to the monitor. "Wait a second."

Sebastian's hand clenches mine harder and we both lean forward.

Doctor Craner lets out a clucking sound as she smacks her lips together. I'm frantically wondering what the hell that means when she smiles broadly and moves her hand to point to the screen. "And there's the other one. Well, look at that. You guys are getting two babies. See here," she points. "The egg split. You're getting identical twins."

"Twins?" Sebastian and I say in unison.

"My dad was a twin," Sebastian replies. "His brother didn't make it."

I drag my eyes from the screen to look up at Sebastian. His jaw is tense, and his eyes don't move from the screen.

"Yep, definitely twins. I can give you some information about multiples. It's nothing to worry about. Your body knows what to do, and the risks of multiples have never been this low," she replies, but it's difficult to take anything in, because, *fuck, I'm having twins*. "Mr Stone, are you okay? You look pale all of a sudden," Doctor Craner asks, her smile fading.

Sebastian doesn't just look pale, he looks terrified.

"I'm fine. I just… It's a baby. Two babies. One, two. Definitely two," he stutters as though the sum of one plus one has him stumped. He still can't seem to drag his eyes from the screen.

"Why don't you get dressed Mum, and I'll take Dad through to the office and get him a glass of water."

When they leave the room I gasp for air. Two little peanuts. Their existence changes everything I thought I knew. Fear, excitement, hope, love—the grip of all my emotions is devastating and incredible and miraculous. I allow a tear to escape my eyes before I compose myself and join Sebastian and the doctor in the adjacent office.

The doctor is perched on her desk when I walk back in, scribbling on some notes attached to a clipboard. I scan the room, but I don't see Sebastian.

"Your husband just stepped outside for a moment. I

think he needed a breath of fresh air. It can be a lot to take in." She smiles casually, as though this is nothing to worry about. "Here's your print out. Your husband has a copy too. And beneath that is some information about multiples and the date and time of your next appointment. If you need to reschedule, call Holly on reception."

Doctor Craner smiles again. I want to scream, "Where the fuck is my husband?" But I don't, because he is not my husband. Right now he's not even present. So instead I thank the doctor and walk out of her office, and down to the car in a daze.

Sebastian isn't in the foyer and when I search outside, I notice his car is gone.

"Looks like it's just you and me, peanuts," I say, clutching my paperwork and rubbing my belly.

Chapter 17
Sebastian

"Thought I'd find you here," Luke says from behind me. "Grace texted me. She asked me to check up on you since your phone is off."

I pull my phone out of my jacket pocket. Damn thing died. "She okay?" I check, looking over my shoulder from my spot on the grass.

"She's fine, I think. She wondered why you disappeared from your date?"

"Date." I chuckle under my breath. "She's pregnant. We were at the doctor's office."

"Fuck." Luke sits next to me on the grass.

"Don't swear, you know Mum doesn't like it." I jut my head at our mother's side of the headstone. Luke doesn't know she hated swearing. Not first-hand, anyway. He remembers nothing about our parents.

Luke strokes the white marble and apologises to Mum, and I throw him a sad smile.

"What are you going to do?"

"We're keeping them."

"Them? As in—"

"Twins," I confirm. No matter how many times I say it, it

still doesn't feel possible. *Twins. Twins. Twins.*

"Fuck! Shit—sorry, Mum." He touches the headstone again. "Twins?"

I nod because I can't trust my voice to sound stable.

"Well, fuck me if you don't have some almighty, impressive sperm you're shooting. I always thought you must fire blanks, what with all the women you bang and not so much as one pregnancy scare. You sure they're yours?" Luke asks.

"Positive. They're mine, I have no doubt." I'm not upset with Luke for asking. If the situation was reversed, I'd be asking the same question. "I'm terrified, Luke. Thoughts I've had before are popping into my head like the world is about to end and there's nothing I can do to protect them. Climate change? Did you know the planet is fucked, and no one is doing anything about it? Did you, Luke? Because I saw this thing on the TV that would make your hair curl. Crime? Crime statistics are out of control. There are people killing others for no fucking reason. Kids are doing drugs, committing suicide and getting trafficked into sex dens. Predators are hunting fucking kids, Luke." His hand lands on my shoulder. Of course, he knows, he's a fucking cop. "Everything has changed, and I don't know how the hell I will keep them safe. Like I wonder if I should take them out of society. Buy an island or some shit, but then you think about their health needs and you realise you have to live not far from a great hospital, and I also read how socialisation for kids is important for their self-esteem and mental health and I'm back to square one. Stuck on earth, surrounded by risks and danger." Luke's firm grip doesn't leave my shoulder, and he doesn't interrupt my rant. "I know I sound like a crazy person, but seeing our peanuts, there on the screen, so delicate and tiny and breakable. Seeing Grace, looking at me, at our babies, her eyes filled with wonder and love—what if I fuck this up? This isn't like everything else; this matters."

"You won't fuck this up. Grace, the woman you love, is by your side. You just show up and do your best."

"What if that's not enough? What if something happens to me?"

"Nothing's going to—" He pauses. He's looking at our parent's headstones, too. "Then I'll help Grace. Anything she needs, I'll be there. I swear to you. I'll do everything in my power to ensure my nieces or nephews thrive." I meet Luke's gaze and know he's serious. "But, it won't come to that. We already had our worst luck and now look at you. You've never been this happy. Well, until right now. This is kind of morbid—but I get it. You're overthinking things. I don't like to blow smoke up your ass, but you're a good guy. I've looked up to you my whole life. You already pretty much parented me. You, Gramps and Betty. And I turned out okay, didn't I?" He pulls a face that makes him look like Sloth from the Goonies, and I chuckle.

"I'm going to fucking ace this, Mum and Dad. You wait and see. There won't be a set of kids on the planet that are happier or more loved than mine, I promise."

Luke's grip turns into a one-armed hug. "You've fucking got this." He grins and I tap him upside the head. "I said no fucking swearing in front of Mum."

He drops his arm and shoulder bumps me. "Don't think I won't put you on your ass just because we're in a graveyard," Luke chides me.

"You couldn't put our Gramps down even if he had both hands tied behind his back." I chuckle.

Luke stops jostling me and his face turns serious. "You told Gramps yet?"

"No. Grace wanted to wait until we saw the doctor."

Luke nods, and a grin lights up his face. "I'm going to be a fucking uncle."

I grin too. "Yep. Don't screw it up." I wink and shoulder bump him.

"Don't you have more important places you should be?" he asks, and suddenly the urgency to be with Grace is acute.

"Fuck. I just left her, standing in the doctor's office on her own. I have to go."

I shoot to my car, yelling into the air, over my shoulder, "I'm going to be a fucking dad!"

"Fuck, yeah. The best!" Luke calls after me.

I plug my phone into the charger, start the car and accelerate out of the car park, then I slow down, because I got to take better care of myself. Grace and peanuts are depending on me. I've already done everything I can to make sure they are well taken care of if anything happens to me, but still, I want to be in their lives. I want to hold Grace's hand as they enter the world and get up in the night to feed them. I want to take them to school and teach them how to take down bullies. Mostly, I want to share every moment with Grace.

As I approach Grace's street, there's a call through the Bluetooth on my car. I answer it immediately, hoping it's Grace.

"Sebastian, is everything okay?" Gramps asks.

"Everything is fucking amazing," I sing, feeling much more positive now that I've dealt with some issues.

"Language, my boy!" Gramps chastises. "Is everything okay with your shares? Mathew just called me, he said you've transferred your Stone Enterprise shares to Grace Harper."

Shit. That travelled fast. There was no way Gramps wouldn't find out, but still, that was fast. The moment I got out of the hospital, I made the call. I had to do something. Something to ensure if I die suddenly without warning, Grace and the kids are looked after.

"I can explain—"

Gramps interrupts. "My dear Sebastian, no need to explain. I think I know exactly what's going on. You found someone you care about more than yourself." The happiness in his voice is obvious. "Enjoy spending time with your future wife. I'll see you at my birthday party tonight."

Gramps hangs up the phone, and the smile doesn't leave my face—until I arrive at Grace's house and see her car isn't there, and then suddenly I have a terrible feeling.

Chapter 18
Grace

After the seventh missed call, I pick up the phone.

"Grace, where are you? I've been worried sick," Sebastian says. He sounds genuine. His voice seems strangled and I feel bad for not picking up sooner. "Listen, I need to see you. I'm sorry for running out on you earlier. There were things I needed to do, but I'm okay now. Better than okay, I'm—"

I cut him off. "I'm fine. Just getting my hair done for the big birthday bash, tonight," I lie. "I'll meet you at your gramps around seven. Okay? Look, I really have to go. I'll see you soon." I hang up the phone even though it hurts like hell to do so.

Since leaving the doctor's office alone, I've collected Geraldine and driven around aimlessly, trying to decide what to do.

I've never seen Sebastian look less than composed and sure of himself. In the doctor's office, he looked like a frightened boy.

Does he regret the decisions that have led to today?

Since my sister suggested I should be cautious of Sebastian's intentions, I've been questioning everything. I didn't see the signs that things were wrong with Sam, and I can't help worrying that history could repeat itself. Despite my concerns, I want to continue living the dream… *or living the lie?*

It's six-fifteen. If I will make it to Arthur's party, I need to get a move on. I drop Geraldine off at Mrs McClusky's and, after ten minutes of subtle hint dropping that her good friend Simon could look after Geraldine while she accompanied me to the party, I leave to go get dressed. My decision is made. I can't give up on the hope of something real with Sebastian, not when I want it this bad. Not now I know how good it feels. And not until I unequivocally know if it's a sham.

**

Mrs McClusky knocks on my door at precisely six-fifty. I thought I'd done a good job of deflecting Mrs McClusky's hints for an invitation to Arthur's party, but obviously not, and so I arrive with a plus one to the party. I just hope Arthur doesn't mind me bringing a seventy-year-old gate-crasher.

The evening is mild, with only the slightest breeze warmed by the low hanging sun. The lawns of the estate are tastefully decorated with open marquees, a dance floor, and enough fairy lights that when the sun sets, the manor house gardens will be transformed into a magical fairy tale.

"My dear, you made it." Arthur walks through the modest crowd of well-wishers and wraps his arm around my shoulder to welcome me. "And you look just a vision."

I thank Arthur for his compliment, even though with my limited time to prepare for tonight, coupled with my absent concentration and underlying nausea, I'm not sure I can agree. The old purple cocktail dress with a sweetheart neckline that I wore for my parents' wedding anniversary dinner four years ago was a last-minute decision. Mostly I was just grateful that it still fit and didn't require pressing.

My hair was only washed the night before, and so I just threw it up in a twist on the top of my head, pulling out a few tendrils to frame my face, and then I finished the look with a coat of mascara and a strappy pair of heels that I'm already regretting wearing.

"Happy birthday, Arthur. You don't look a day over fifty," I say, kissing his cheek.

"Come. Your parents and sister are here." Shocked, I allow him to guide me through the party, and Mrs McClusky follows. I wasn't aware they were coming and wonder if the invitation was presented to my dad during their game of golf. If there's one thing my dad never turns down, it's the excuse for a party. "Sebastian is with the caterers. He should be out in a moment. I know he is eager to see you."

I nod. Arthur is a kind-hearted man who cares deeply for his grandson, but he wouldn't be so sure Sebastian was keen to see me had he watched the colour drain from his grandson's face this morning.

I greet Mum and Dad, nestling myself on one of the free, ornate iron chairs beside them. In the corner of the largest marquee, a band plays a classical composition. There must be a hundred people here, but I can't see Sebastian yet.

Mrs McClusky swipes two glasses of champagne from the tray of a uniformed server and then sits beside me, and my dad throws me a mischievous smirk as we watch Mrs McClusky quaff both the glasses in quick succession.

"Gosh, I was thirsty. Grace, can you see if you can catch me another glass? My legs aren't what they were, and I don't think I've got the stamina to be chasing those waiters around," Mrs McClusky slides me an empty champagne flute and then whispers, "even if they have got cute little tight buns."

I let out a chortle even though my stomach is knotted with nerves. I've never seen Mrs McClusky drunk. This could be interesting.

When I return with a tray of champagne and an orange juice for me, Sebastian and Luke are sitting at our table. My parents are laughing at something one of them said, and even my sister seems to have warmed to the two brothers. Since Mrs McClusky hasn't moved, Sebastian, and I end up separated by Mrs McClusky. Not for long, as Sebastian immediately gets out of his seat and walks to my side, perching in between Mrs McClusky and I. He takes my left hand and kisses my palm. "You look sensational. I've missed you today." Then he kisses my lips and my heart rate goes crazy.

"Ah. You two are just adorable," my mum says, and rubs her hands in glee.

Sebastian throws my mum a grin and then asks me to dance. He leads me to the dance floor, which takes a while because everyone wants to stop and talk to him. He introduces me as his fiancée, which I don't mind, even though the status of our engagement isn't confirmed.

I'm already getting drawn into the bubble that is being with Sebastian. He wraps his arms around my waist as mine latch onto his neck and then he leans down and whispers close to my ear, "I'm sorry I left you today."

"That's okay. It was an emotional day," I reply.

"It wasn't okay. Deserting you. Not. Okay. Not okay by a straight mile. I got spooked. My head was swimming with thoughts, and I needed to get everything straight in my head. I'm happy, Grace. Happier than I have ever been. And I will never skip out on you ever again. I promise."

His eyes fix on mine with a look of sheer adoration. When he looks at me this way, it's impossible not to believe him. Of course he's spooked. I'm spooked too.

"I forgive you."

"I fucking love you. I love you so much it hurts. And I can't wait to bring these babies into the world with you." Sebastian's smiling now. Not just smiling, but grinning his face off, and it's catching.

"I fucking love you, too," I repeat his sentiment and his lips come crashing down on mine. And just like that, it doesn't matter that he left me at the doctor's office. It doesn't matter that it has clouded my judgement with doubt, because I love him, pure and simple.

When another couple clear their throats close to us, we break apart and join my family at the table. Mrs McClusky has emptied another two glasses of champagne and has sent Luke off to fetch more.

The evening is alive with dancing, laughter and the finest food being served to everyone at decorated tables. My mother and father seem to make friends with a half the crowd who are eager to meet Sebastian's future bride. In this setting, everything feels real. Sebastian's feelings for me, his family's acceptance that I will join them, and most of all the validity of our relationship. It paints a happy future. One in which our children will be surrounded by love and want for nothing.

As the night draws to a close, and Mrs McClusky is ushered from her spot twirling circles on the dance floor, the band stop playing and then Arthur takes the mic on the stage, and thanks everyone for sharing his birthday with him. Everyone breaks into a chorus of Happy Birthday, and when they are done, and three cheers have been bellowed by the crowds, Arthur asks Sebastian to join him on the stage.

"Brother, the caterers want paying and I haven't got my wallet," Luke asks Sebastian before he gets out of his seat. Sebastian pulls out his wallet and hands Luke his credit card, placing his wallet on the table and then leaves to go join his grandfather on stage.

The crowd applauds. Together, standing side by side, it's easy to see the likeness between them. Both tall, commanding with their presence. Impeccably dressed, as always, in sharp suits and crisp shirts. Looking at Arthur is like getting a glimpse of Sebastian in years to come. It's a handsome vision.

"Sebastian Stone. My grandson, my friend. You and your brother are like sons to me. Luke, my darling boy, where is he? Come up here, boy."

Mrs McClusky digs her elbow into my side, and rambles that the waiter has missed our table. I try to ignore her and listen intently to Arthur as Luke joins the stage.

"Luke, a man of the law. A pillar of society. A man of his word. With his focus and commitment, he is an inspiration to all. Sebastian, my dear son. Always my shadow. Always keen to follow in my footsteps at Stone Enterprises. He has worked sixty-hour weeks since he joined the company and has made many excellent business deals that men with twice his experience would struggle to pull off. Sebastian, in case you haven't all heard, has gotten engaged to the beautiful and sweet Grace Harper." He raises his whiskey glass to the crowd, and they cheer. I blush and shush Mrs McClusky, who is pulling on my arm. "I love you both. Grace is a creative woman with a caring, nurturing nature. She is exactly what my grandson needs and deserves, and I cannot wait to see them married, for they will make a fine couple." Arthur continues, but Mrs McClusky is babbling and waving Sebastian's wallet in front of my face so I can't see or hear properly. I pull the wallet out of her hand and place it back on the table.

When I look back up, Sebastian has a mic too. The grin on his face is up to his ears. "Arthur Stone, Gramps. It's hard to believe you are eighty today. You have been the father, guardian, and friend that we lost. You and Betty taught us love, honour and respect. On this, your eightieth year, I want to make it known, in case I don't say it often enough, that Luke and I love and cherish you. A fierce business man, but more importantly, a loving family man. I strive to achieve your same level of significance to those around me." Sebastian sounds choked up and I'm forced to wipe away a tear. "Particularly now Grace and I will be parents. That's right. Please, everyone, bring your hands together for my amazing fiancée, Grace. This woman has given me the world, and I cannot even describe the depth of my feelings for her. She is everything."

I hear my mother's sharp intake of breath before the

crowd goes wild. Mrs McClusky almost falls off her chair as she tries to hug and kiss me and on the stage, Sebastian looks happy, elated even, that is until his eyes find mine and he realises I might just kill him for outing our secret on the stage before I even told my sister and parents.

Flo gasps. "Orange juice! I should have bloody-well known." She veers around the table and she and my mum and dad envelope me and Mrs McClusky, who sticks to my side, in a tight hug.

"I can't believe it. I'll be a nanna." My mum cries happy tears and my dad clutches my hand, trying not to cry but failing.

"Twins," I whisper and my mum's mouth pops open.

"Grace. My darling. Oh my darling, this is wonderful. You must come up for the weekend. I'm so excited I want to hear everything. I promise not to interfere, but babies. We'll have babies in the family again."

Even though I'm furious at Sebastian, seeing my family so happy is the best feeling in the entire world. There were times in our past I thought my family would never smile again. Now, the pain we've all been through feels so distant; it was like it happened to someone else.

On the stage, Arthur is hugging his grandsons, and the crowd are still applauding. Mrs McClusky accosts a passing waitress and quaffs another glass of champagne, then her eyes look down at the table, fixing on a rectangle of paper hanging out of Sebastian's wallet, but my attention is diverted to Arthur who is wiping his eyes with a handkerchief.

"I'm a very old man. An old man who wondered if he'd ever live to see the next generation of Stone's. Grace and Sebastian, you have made me so proud. So unbelievably happy. Sebastian, you will be an incredible father, and the perfect person to take charge of Stone Enterprises."

Sebastian shakes his head and looks confused.

Mrs McClusky is flapping a sheet of paper in front of my face, and I swat it away like an annoying fly.

"That's right, Sebastian. As of today, I'm handing over the reins of Stone Enterprises and gifting you my 51 percent share. You're a family man now, and also, you're ready. Of course, you would have owned all of the company had you not made a sizeable gift of your own shares, but that was just one of the many ways you have shown me that your heart has grown."

I'm not sure who Sebastian gave his shares to, he's never mentioned parting with shares, but seeing his face light up with emotion and pride with the realisation of his grandfather's gift and his praise of the man he has become makes my own heart fill with love and pride. In fact, the more I've gotten to know Sebastian, the more I've wondered if his yearning for the company had more to do with knowing he had earned his grandfather's trust and confidence as a businessman, than being the majority shareholder and getting to call the shots.

Arthur wraps an arm around Sebastian, and Luke is shaking his hand so hard I wonder if Sebastian's arm is in danger of popping out of its socket. Sebastian's expression is pure shock. He looks overwhelmed, the colour has drained from his face and it reminds me of his face in the doctor's office. I want to go to him, hold him tight and congratulate him, but Mrs McClusky is in my damned way, still flapping a sheet of paper.

"What is it Mrs McClusky?" I bark, allowing my annoyance to get the better of my composure.

"This fell out of Sebastian's wallet."

I sigh. Take the sheet of paper and start to fold it into a shape that will fit in his wallet when I notice the heading: *Operation: My Fake Girlfriend.*

My eyes scan to each of the bullet points written in Sebastian's handwriting beneath the heading.

Find a chick who is into me (she has to be hot!)
Stage a cute first meeting
Post a ton of dates on social media with puke-inducing photos
Show an interest in what's important to her

Bring her to family Sunday with Gramps
Propose
Gramps thinks I'm a one-woman man and hands over the business.

"I can't believe I got everything I ever wanted," Sebastian says and the words reverberate around the room.

Everything he always wanted.

The air is sucked from my lungs, and suddenly I can't breathe. It feels like my dress is too tight and my airway too small.

"Grace, honey. Are you okay?" Mum asks.

I drop the toxic sheet of paper as if letting it go will relieve me of my symptoms.

"I'm fine. I'm going to the bathroom."

I shake off Mrs McClusky, grab my clutch, and attempt to stomp through the throng of well-wishers. Every time another person stands in my way to congratulate me, the space gets smaller until I'm barging people out of my way. Even once I am outside, surrounded by cooler, fresher air, I still don't feel far enough away. That's when I spot my car, and the solution to my predicament.

Run.

Chapter 19
Sebastian

By the time I get back to where Grace was sitting, she is gone.

Shit.

She's angry I announced the pregnancy.

I don't know what came over me, but standing up there, surrounded by friends and family, I was so happy I could have burst. I wanted to scream it from the rooftops, but now I'm back on earth, pangs of regret are pummelling my gut like a bad case of the shits.

"Congratulations, son." Grace's dad shakes my hand. "I guess this really is welcome to the family." Grace's mum stands from her seat and hugs me. A warm embrace that when she pulls away reveals the depth of her emotion. Her eyes are moist, and mascara has leaked beneath her eyes.

"Mrs Harper. I'm sorry. I shouldn't have announced it like that. I got swept away. Again. The engagement and now this. Fuck—shit, sorry, I didn't mean to swear." I tug at my hair.

When did I become such a fucking liability?

"That's okay, Sebastian. Sounds to me like you got swept away by my daughter." She smiles knowingly and leans into my ear. "But you might want to go find her and straighten this out. She was a little… shocked. I'm sure she'll forgive you." She winks, and I could pick her up and kiss her for the reassuring pep talk and vote of confidence.

"I'm going. Which direction did she go?"

Mrs Harper points and I take a step around McClusky, but her fingernails latch into my arm, through my suit jacket.

"You dropped this, and your wallet. I tried to give it to Grace but she just read it and stormed off. Always in a hurry that girl and didn't even check to see if I needed a refill before she left. Could you be a dear and see if they've got any brandy behind the bar? Champagne brings on my migraines."

McClusky continues to chatter. I take a step away and my eyes lock on the sheet of paper. The paper that about a month ago I jotted down some stupid ideas to secure something that doesn't even seem important now.

"You actual dickhead!" Flo says from beside me, her eyes locked on the sheet of paper in my hands. "I'm going to kick your ass."

"I won't stop you." I shake my head. "I wrote this before. This isn't the plan anymore. It's not the plan at all," I repeat. White noise filters through my ears and in and out of my lungs as though the world has ceased to exist. If I've lost Grace, if she's read this and believes I've been faking my feelings for her to get the business, then my greatest fear has come true; I've lost everything.

"What the fuck were you thinking?" Flo shoves me with her palm to my shoulder, and I walk in the direction she pushes me until we are outside. "Are you out of your mind treating my sister like this?" Flo isn't just angry. She's incensed and looks like she wants to spill blood. My blood.

My Gramps saunters outside, as though he's been looking for me. He smiles, but then registers the look on my face. "Sebastian. What's wrong? I thought you'd be happy. You got the company." He takes a step closer and greets Flo. "Having said that, you barely own much more than you did now that you gave all your shares to Grace."

"You gave Grace your shares in Stone Enterprises. Why?" Flo asks.

"In case anything happened to me. I needed to know they'd all be okay. But she's gone. I've lost her."

There's a grave look on Flo's face, and my Gramps remains eerily silent. So silent I can hear the crickets chorus over the band playing inside the marquee.

"Then you need to go after her," my gramps finally says. "Whatever you've done, undo it. Fix it. If you've loved her hard enough, she will believe you're sorry."

In a state of shock, I head towards my car. What if it's too late?

"Wait!" Flo calls. "I might have contributed to this mess."

I turn back and study her face. How has she added to my idiocy?

She screws up her nose in a sheepish apology. "The way you guys started dating. The fake girlfriend to convince your gramps you were a changed man, and then actually changing. It seemed to be too good to be true. The only way Grace would have entertained a future with you in the first place was if it stood no chance of lasting. She dates guys she knows won't settle down. She had a Tinder page that would scare off every guy within a hundred-mile radius. She fears getting attached, and that's probably my fault. She had to say goodbye to me six different times. But I got through it. I lived. But Grace, I don't think she ever got over the fear. Now, if she gets spooked, she runs. And believe me, she is spooked. She's spooked because she knows this is real."

"Sounds like someone else I know," Gramps muses.

"Gramps, I'm sorry. It seemed like the answer, but it wasn't. It was… stupid."

Gramps laughs. "You don't think I knew this was a rouse at the start? But, I took one look at Grace's face in your Instagram post, she looked like a woman in love, and I knew there's no way you'd be safe from a love like that. I didn't know it would play out like this, but I hoped it would. And then today, when you transferred your shares, I knew you were ready to be the head of Stone Enterprises. You finally have something that means more to you than just a business. Actually, you have three things. Three things to fight for, and to thrive for. I'm proud of you, son. Now, go find Grace and throw yourself on her mercy."

I don't wait to be told twice. I run to my car, fumbling for my keys and praying to God that I can make Grace understand that I love her.

Chapter 20
Grace

I load my suitcase into the back of my car, hoping it has everything I need for at least a week. Although, my eyes are so wet, I'm not sure what I packed or if it will be enough to last me. Luckily, at my parents' house there's still a wardrobe full of crap I owned before I moved out at the end of my teens. If I need to squeeze into my old school uniform, I'm sure I can let it out and make do. Anything to get some space and clear my head.

With the suitcase packed, I grab Geraldine's carrier and cluck my tongue to let him know it's time to go.

Shit, Geraldine. I don't have time for this. Where are you?

My cat, pissed off at having been left with Mrs McClusky's friend, Simon, is nowhere to be seen, despite the open tin of tuna I am waving around and gagging on in equal amounts. As soon as we got in, he ran right into the bedroom and hid under the bed, but since I've been in and out of every room throwing things in a suitcase, he could have migrated to any part of the house, including out the door.

Double shit.

The door is wide open.

Geraldine is not inside.

This tin of tuna is going to make me puke if I don't put it down.

I put the open tin of tuna in the entry to the door and go outside, calling his name nicely, like I'm not planning on making a cardigan out of his fur. That's when I hear the obnoxious sound of a car racing down the street and screeching to a halt outside my place.

I call Geraldine again. Louder this time, while looking around the plant pots where he sometimes likes to take a shit.

Sebastian slams his car door, but I remain focused on my task, climbing over the picket fence to check if he's got into next door's porch.

"Grace, wait. Be careful, you might fall." He races after me, but I ignore him and carry on with my mission. Him on one side, me on the other, probably just like it's always been. "Why did you go? I mean, I know why you went, but I can explain. I didn't plan to out the babies during my speech…." His voice trails off as his eyes meet my glare.

I look away, check the porch and there is no sign of Geraldine. I have no choice but to cross the fence again into Sebastian's path if I am going to catch my cat. I consider how much I still like my cat, which isn't a lot right now, but still, I'll regret leaving him to fend for himself if I leave without him.

I mutter as I head back to my side of the fence. "Always full of ideas and explanations, aren't you, Sebastian? Let's go back to your place. Let's fake a relationship. Let's fake getting engaged on social media. Let's run out and leave my FAKE fiancée at the clinic." I cock my leg over the fence which is only thigh high, but I'm still wearing my long purple satin frock, so it isn't as easy as it looks. "Let's tell the entire party I knocked up Grace, that way Gramps will surely hand over the Stone legacy." My heel hitches on the horizontal baseboard, and Sebastian's hand grasps my hand to steady me. His touch sends a bolt of electricity straight to my heart. It feels good, but it also hurts like hell. "Don't touch me!" I fling away his hand and use both my hands to hold the fence and unsnag my heel. My dress splits farther up my thigh as I kick my leg back over to my side where I storm away from Sebastian towards the back of my house. "Gerry. Geraldine. Here kitty."

Sebastian calls for the cat too, but I throw him a death stare. "I actually want my cat to come back. Stop calling him, you'll make him go away. You on the other hand, you can go away."

"Grace. Let me explain."

I walk away from him, into the back garden to check the shed. Sebastian follows.

"I should never have written that list. It was an info dump of ideas I wrote when frustrated and trying to think of solutions. I do that sometimes. But as soon as I wrote them, I stuffed the sheet inside my wallet and I swear I didn't look at them again. I certainly wasn't following them like some kind of fucked up to-do list."

I open the shed and check behind the mower. Geraldine isn't in here. I close the door and work my way around the house.

"I spoke to your mum and dad. They're happy you're pregnant. I think your sister is too. And I told them I'm sorry for announcing it at the party. I'd been holding everything in. And I missed you all day. I was desperate to put the image of our babies onto Instagram and shout it out to the world, but I didn't, because I wanted to wait until you were ready for us to share it."

Sebastian throws me a pleading smile.

"So you think I should be grateful that you refrained from sharing our news with the entire world before I even told my family? You think that because you only shared it with a hundred people at a party, I should pat you on the back?" My voice has hitched, and even I can hear the anger in my voice, which isn't like me, but the emotions of the past few days is like a boiler inside me and it's about to go off.

I walk back around the building, to my front door.

"No. You should be angry. I fucked up. I was so fucking happy, and I was just bursting to tell everyone. I've never been this happy. It took me by surprise and—"

"You mean you finally got what you wanted. I've got to say, the engagement was a good one. You even made me feel like that one was for me, but announcing the babies? How could a family man like your gramps possibly resist giving you everything when you revealed that? All this time I thought there was an us," I gesture from him to me, "but there was just you and an empire, and I want nothing to do with any of it." I pause in the doorway. The hall light is throwing just enough light on to Sebastian's face that I can see the hurt look in his eyes. At that moment, Geraldine lurches out from beneath my Juniper bush and runs across the lawn, leaping straight into Sebastian's arms like a geriatric turncoat. I stroke him once, glad to have found him, then pick up his carrier and hold it out for Sebastian to put him inside. He strokes him head to tail and nuzzles him. The sight makes my throat hurt when I swallow.

He puts Gerry into the carrier and I pull my front door shut, lock it, and walk to my car, avoiding Sebastian's searching gaze because of the very real fear that one locked-on look in his eyes and I'll fall to pieces. Once Gerry is safely on the back seat, I walk around my car and my hand pauses on the driver's door.

Sebastian follows me. "I didn't make us engaged for the right reasons. I admit that. I was selfish and jealous and I wanted you free of your ex. You didn't need me for that. Hell, you don't need me for anything, but I know you want me. Even if your instinct is to run, I'm begging you to reconsider and stay because I love you. I feel it. I've never felt anything like what I feel for you and it's making me crazy. Since I've met you I've felt fear, real honest to God terror at the thought of everything that could go wrong but the high of being with you is so fucking high I can't let go.

Not unless you tell me I have to." I stare at the floor, torn in two between running and staying. Seconds pass. He must read the pained look on my face as I try to commit to my decision to run because, with resignation he asks, "Where will you go?"

"I'm going to go stay with my parents for a while. I need to figure out where I go next." My voice doesn't sound like mine. My throat is numb, like all of my nerves shot into my head and heart to ache and sting as though physical symptom of leaving Sebastian—acute to the point of pain.

"Please don't go. Don't run."

"I'm not running," I dismiss.

"You sure? Because it looks a lot like running away from over here."

I turn and look at him. Tall. Thick, broad shoulders. Designer suit. Dark, thick, shiny hair, just the right length to slide my fingers into and grip it hard. Masculine face, chiselled, perfectly proportioned and so mouth-wateringly handsome it hurts my eyes to look away.

"You broke my heart" is all I can choke out.

"You broke mine too by saying you're leaving."

"Why? In case your gramps takes the company back."

"I don't care about the company. I did, but it pales to how much I care about you and our babies. I make mistakes, Grace. I run when I should walk, and I jump when I should probably duck, and since I met you, I have been running and jumping like a madman. But it's because I love you." I hear a pained sigh leave his lips. "But you run too. And right now, I know you don't want to. I wrote that damned list. I did it because I was single-minded in what I wanted, but now my priorities have shifted. I'm still single-minded in what I want, and it's you." I let go of the car door and turn to him. I want to trust him so much my chest feels like it's about to explode. His eyes pin me to the spot with their intensity. He takes a step closer, and my knees weaken. "I wrote a new plan." His hand reaches into his pocket and pulls out a sheet of paper. "This morning, all I could think about was the loss of my parents and how I had to do everything I could to make sure you and our children had security. I was lucky, I had my gramps. I had Betty. My parent's made provisions. I needed to do that too. Read it."

He holds his hand out, the paper flaps in the breeze.

I hold out my hand and take it. He's less than a foot away and the wind is blowing his scent right into my lungs, enveloping me in a deep sense of safety and love. My eyes fix on his, and I wonder why I'm running when everything I want is standing in front of me.

"I was waiting for this to go wrong. As soon as it became real, I was sure it would go wrong."

"I know." I always knew he was afraid to fall in love. It's one of the reasons I thought I'd be safe with him.

My eyes flick down to his list.

Operation: Marry Grace

Compromise. She is right more often than I am

Housing. If Grace wants, we can live in her house. It's a great street for raising a family

Communicate. Grace deserves someone who listens

Teach her the only place she need run is into my arms. I am here for her, and I am not going away

Put my shares of Stone Enterprises into her name. That way if anything ever happens to me, she will have security, always

Marry Grace, the only woman I ever loved

"You'd do this for me?" I ask, but even as I do, I know that he would. Sebastian has always shown me generosity and kindness, and deep down, I know he loves me. It's the main reason walking away from him is so painful.

"I already did. As of this morning, you own 49 percent of Stone Enterprises. As of about an hour ago, I own 51 percent, but I'll gladly even that up. I'll give up the business to prove it to you. I'd give anything. When I left the clinic this morning, I brainstormed everything I could think of to make you my wife because I love you. I know you said you're not ready, and I know we're still figuring things out, and you're learning to trust me, but I already know, we were made for each other. The list probably isn't complete but I'm going to work on being the best partner, husband, father—" A tear leaks down my face and Sebastian's hand reaches out to stop its path. "Don't cry. If you need space, I'll give you space, but please don't leave."

In front of me is the sweetest, most handsome, generous, and caring man. The father of my babies. The man who offered me one night, then a month, then the rest of my life. He is flawed, but then so am I.

My feet feel rooted to the floor and the thought of getting in my car causes more tears to escape from my eyes. "I'm not going."

"Thank you."

"I'm staying. But only if you'll stay with me?"

Sebastian shakes his head as though he doesn't understand and takes a step closer until our chests are almost touching. "You mean?" His brows furrow as he waits for me to confirm what I mean.

"We might both end up broken-hearted, but it's worth the risk. You are worth the risk. My fears were wrong. You care about me. More than that, you love me and I love you."

Sebastian's arms wrap around my waist and he pulls me in and picks me up, lifting me high until my lips meet his. I fling my arms around him, pulling myself into him until there are no gaps and all of me touches all of him. My mouth opens to welcome his tongue and my heart gallops from our contact. I love this man. Every fibre of my body is screaming that he is mine and I am his, and together we are meant to be. My hands shimmy between the fabric of his shirt and his belt until they latch onto his smooth, hard skin. God, I have missed him.

Too soon, he lowers me until my feet touch the floor and pulls away.

"There's one more thing." He shakes his head. "Two if you include the other thing." He sheepishly pulls his mouth into a lopsided line.

"What have you done now?"

"I… well, technically, this was a business move, so you can't be mad with me. Shit, well you can, but I didn't want you to miss out." He must read from my face that I have no clue where he is going with this, so he continues, "I instructed Mathew to patent *Graceful Designs*. You have the domain name, the warehouse premises, and the office space. As it takes off, and it will, you can move the premises wherever you want. But for now, I hope you'll take the office next to mine?"

"What? We're in business?!" I let out a shrill of excitement and throw my arms back around Sebastian. I knew the contracts had gone off to Mathew to be finalised but so much has been going on I wasn't sure what would become of it all. "Thank you. Thank you. Thank you."

Sebastian's face is lit up with happiness, crinkling the corners of his eyes and flashing his perfect teeth.

"Now might not be the time to remind you, but now that we're going to be working together I fully expect to cash in our agreement."

"What agreement?" I release him and step back to gauge his face, wondering if baby brain is an actual thing this early in the pregnancy.

"Blinds down. Lunch date. No food. My desk."

A thrill of excitement zings up my spine, and I launch myself at Sebastian with the power of a rocket. Flinging my hands into his hair and my lips down on his. A minute later, I break our kiss.

"What was the other thing?" I ask curiously.

"You really want it?"

"Oh, I want it all right."

"Okay. You got it. I was going to wait and do this. Do it in a more romantic setting, with flowers and food, and six months under our belts, but I can't wait. I'll wait if you want to, but I need to do this now. I need you to know. You already got the ring, but I want to make things official. I want to do it for real, and I want you to know that I mean it." Sebastian gets down on one knee and I feel the air whoosh from my lungs as I let out a gasp.

"Grace Harper, love of my life. Sexiest, smartest woman in the world and mother to be of the most amazing two kids out there. It still thrills me to say it. You're already my business partner, be my partner in life, my partner in crime, just my partner, marry me?"

The decision is simple. I already know that I love him. I think I've known for a while, since he turned up at my place with a simple gift that summed me up perfectly. And a sexy smile. A part of me knows I can trust him, even if this is unchartered waters. I need to take a leap of faith, but I'm doing it with conviction that he won't hurt me.

"Yes. I'll marry you."

Sebastian rockets me up in the air and Geraldine squawks like a pissed-off parrot from inside the car.

"You won't regret it!" He spins me around and then brings me back down to earth for a kiss. "You, me, Gerry, and the peanuts are going to be the happiest people in the whole of Heaven. Well, apart from Gramps, that is. I think he'll probably be so happy we better get an ambulance on standby in case his heart gives out." Sebastian throws me a sexy wink and puts me down, drawing me into one of his standout, sexy kisses and making my heart rate skyrocket.

"We are. I have faith. Let's go inside, there's something I want to show you."

Sebastian reaches into the back of my car, grabs Gerry and my suitcase, and then he takes hold of my hand and I lead him inside our home where we let Gerry at the tuna, and I show Sebastian just how much I missed him.

Epilogue
Luke

The little white chapel at Heaven, East Angleford is nestled between two vineyards. Remote, and picturesque, it's where my parents got married, and also where they are buried. Before we go to take our places at the front of the church, Seb and I take two extra button-hole, white roses to their headstones.

"Wish you could have seen this, Mum and Dad," Seb says, placing a rose on each side of the double white marble headstone.

"They're watching. I can feel it," I reply. "It sounds corny, but I can. They're here, and they're so fucking proud of you."

Seb's fist flies out and knocks into my shoulder, sending me off balance. "Don't fucking swear in front of Mum and Dad."

I shove him back. "Don't you fucking swear in front of Mum and Dad, then."

Seb grabs my jacket and I grab his.

"Oh, you want to go do you brother on your wedding day? That's fine, you got it. But don't blame me if Grace busts your ass for having a black eye in the wedding shots!"

Seb's face breaks into a grin and he lets go of me, brushing down the front of his suit jacket to straighten it. Then he reaches out and adjusts the rose in my button hole. "Come on, Luke. Let's go hand over my freedom."

"You've got this. Grace is the woman you didn't know you were waiting for." I throw him a grin and clap him on the back. "Just a shame you got to her first." I dig him in the ribs, hard enough for him to feel it, not hard enough that he'll dig me back.

"Fuck. I'm getting married. We're having twins. And I never felt this fucking excited."

Hearing Seb talk this way is a new development. He swore off relationships his whole life in the belief that happiness always went wrong. Hearing him embrace this new future has me choked up and feeling all sorts of pride at how far he's come.

"You deserve it, brother. Let's go wait for your woman."

We head to the alter, and Seb sweats as he waits for Grace to arrive. It's my job to stand beside him looking hot and to keep watch for Grace's friend's kid, Jessica, who is the flower girl and then make sure Seb is standing in the right place as Grace walks down the aisle. But my eyes keep flitting to Rosie, my brother's PA, who sits two rows back. All on her own, with no plus one, she looks hot as fuck, and not just because it is mid-summer and the temperature is roasting. Her hair is swept over one shoulder, revealing a long neck with soft skin that I wouldn't mind nipping with my teeth. Even though my attention is on Rosie, I can't fail to notice the glances and glares of some of the other single women of Heaven. Half the females from my high school are here and many of them have been in my bed, on the seats of my BMW, in the canteen of our school, with me, naked.

It's not like I set out to sleep with so many women in Heaven—and I've always been straight with them. I am not looking for a relationship. I work long hours. I do a dangerous job that could get me killed. I know the risks, and

I accept them. I wouldn't make a woman take on that kind of risk, though. They always agree. Like, "Yeah, Luke. I just want some fun." But they always change their minds right after and start messaging me for another date or just one more hook-up. Now, standing up here, with all their eyes on me, Seb isn't the only one sweating.

When little Jessica walks in and gives me a thumbs up, the whole congregation stands and the wedding music plays. Grace opted for the Mendelssohn's "Wedding March"—I say Grace, because I think Seb would have married her to "Baby Shark" if she'd wanted. He's got it so bad, but it looks good on him. It looks good on both of them.

The congregation as a whole gasps when she walks through the door in a full-length, silky white dress that trails all the way to the door from the middle of the aisle. Her baby bump is only slightly noticeable beneath the material. She's carrying white roses and a few are plaited into her dark hair which trails down her back. I don't know much about bridal fashion, but she looks breathtaking. Grace's eyes fix on Seb. She looks a mixture of hungry, like she wants to eat him, and emotional, like she might cry. Seb's grin is a reassuring-cat-that-got-the-cream. Any trace of nerves he had are gone, replaced with contented certainty. He's getting married to the woman he loves, and the mixture of emotions on his face makes me certain no one ever felt as fucking fortunate as he does in this moment.

My eyes flick over to Rosie. We met for the first time this morning, and she made it imminently clear she's heard the rumours about me and won't be giving me the time of day. She's wearing a slight frown as she spots me watching her; it's almost camouflaged by her delicate smile. I wonder if she likes weddings. Most women seem to, though she has certainly not conformed to what I know about most women. For one, she seems immune to my charms. It's making me more intrigued, if only because she carries a lick of trouble about her. I make a mental note to keep an eye on her. Since she's pretty easy on the eyes, it shouldn't be too hard.

Pastor Dean is an old man with no hair and skin like a raisin. He knows everyone in the town and has married generations of locals, including my parents. He holds Grace and Sebastian's hands as he welcomes them to the front, but they don't notice him, so focused on each other. They cling to the other so tightly, it almost feels voyeuristic to watch.

Once the pastor orders us to be seated, he reads from his book and I tune him out a bit. Weddings have never really been my thing. Besides, my attention keeps wandering to the woman two rows back. I covertly look over my shoulder a few times and when I do, she is staring at me. I throw her a wink that confirms I caught her checking me out, but she only returns a bored eye-roll. That's until my gramps nudges me and tells me to stop fooling around and pay attention.

When Sebastian reads his vows, the entire room falls silent. I swear every woman in Heaven's ovaries swell at the promises he makes to their unborn children. Then he pulls a list out of his pocket and I shake my head and face palm. It's his love of lists that almost stopped today from ever happening.

"This all began with a simple list I like to call O.M.G. Operation Marry Grace." When he speaks, it's only to Grace, like the church isn't packed with people. "I've learned a lot about myself since I met you. You've taught me a lot too. Like I can be bull-headed and I need to slow down, listen and compromise. Compromise, because you tend to be right more often than I am. We will raise a family, together, because family is all that matters in the end. You are my family. I promise to communicate, because you deserve someone who listens, and in turn I vow to be your haven. The only place you ever need run, is into my arms. And I will provide security, so that if anything ever happens to me, you and our babies will be safe, always. I promise to cherish you, Grace, the only woman I ever loved, the only woman I ever will love."

Fuck. Turns out my brother has a heart in there that is beating like a fucking wrecking ball for his woman. I wonder what it's like to feel that kind of emotion. That kind of responsibility for another person's happiness. I swallow down a lump as Grace begins her vows.

"Sebastian. You came into my life during the storm and quickly became my sunshine. You taught me to be brave and stand up for myself, but you also taught me that fear has its place too. The fear of what we have at stake makes our love and the lives we've created more precious, more important than our solitary goals. You have shown me that I am strong, but that together we are stronger, and I promise to lean on you when times get tough, and my God, with two babies I know they will." Grace tinkles a laugh and so does the audience, but I'm too choked to pay attention, because Seb is so enrapt with Grace, so utterly devoted to every word she speaks, I'm rooted to the spot with bated breath, hanging onto her every word and moved by the way Seb clutches her hands as though she is everything. "But I know we will cherish the good times, the taste of sweet ice cream and sun on our skin, because with you in our lives, I know they will be plentiful. Sebastian Stone, I take you as my husband, my friend, and my equal. All that we face, we will face together."

The crowd claps as my brother and his wife kiss, and all of a sudden I'm finding it difficult to fucking swallow so I let out a cough and check behind me for a distraction. Rosie gives Mrs McClusky's shoulder a squeeze and hands her a tissue. The old lady seems emotional, but this is mitigated by the reverberating sound of a loud loogie getting blown into the tissue. Beside McClusky, I try to read Rosie's face. I'm good with reading people, it's one of the reasons I'm an excellent cop. But I can't get a read on her, and it's frustrating the hell out of me.

With the rings in place on Seb and Grace's fingers, the crowd hollers and cheers and throw rice over the couple as they walk out of the church to begin their new lives together. When the whole place resembles something out of a carb-lovers dream and the cars arrive to ferry everyone to the reception, I congratulate my brother. Even though it was just a few words, a few fancy dresses, I can tell a transformation has taken place. His future is now Grace and their babies, and it makes me wonder what my own will look like.

Of course, first, I must deal with my imminent future: surviving a wedding reception stuffed with more of my previous hook-ups than can possibly be good for my health. That, and my brother's hot PA—the mysterious new chick in town who already hates my guts—sitting right next to me throughout the duration of the meal and speeches. This is going to be a difficult, possibly painful night. Thank God the bar is free and it's open until midnight.

The End

Coming Soon~ Luke and Rosie's story:
Sexy With Attitude Too (SWAT)

Acknowledgements

THANK YOU to everyone who read this book and for all the support and love shown for the crazy characters I invent. Nothing thrills me more than cruising Amazon and reading all the brilliant reviews and logging into my email to find a note of thanks from someone who enjoyed one of my books. You guys rock!

I definitely could not have finished this book without the help of Randie Creamer, my editor. Thank you for all your support and friendship and also for being so brilliant at your job. When I think back how many years have passed and how many books you have helped me finish, I can't decide if you are due parole or a medal! Thanks so much for sticking with me <3

The legendary Ellen Montoya! Thank you for your friendship and the countless hours of your time you have so selflessly lent to me. One day, in a bar near you, I will repay your kindness and I cannot wait for that day.

To Ana Rita Clemente, you have been a friend and font of advice during truly testing times. A busy mum, and a fellow bookworm, the time you have lent me has been so generous. A friend for life!

Gina Putvain, another friend who has stuck by me and my writing for a long time. Despite being super busy, Gina is always gracious with her time and expertise and for that I will always adore her.

Thank you, Ann Bang, thank you for lending me your eagle-eyes and helping me make my books better.

Laura Burton, my friend, my colleague, my fellow lunatic – I love you!

About the Author

Emily James is a British author who lives on the south coast of England. She loves to travel and enjoys nothing more than a great romance story. On the rare occasions that she hasn't got her nose in a book, Emily likes to spend time with her beautiful family and friends.

You can be notified of Emily's future projects via her mailing list:

http://eepurl.com/cpN4t1

Find her on Facebook:

https://www.facebook.com/emily.james.author

Or email her at: emilyjames.author@gmail.com

Operation: My Fake Girlfriend

Ingram Content Group UK Ltd.
Milton Keynes UK
UKHW041543300623
424357UK00001B/10